JO SANDHU

TARIN OF THE MAMMOTHS

The Exile

PUFFIN BOOKS

PUFFIN BOOKS

UK | USA | Canada | Ireland | Australia
India | New Zealand | South Africa | China

Penguin Books is part of the Penguin Random House group of companies
whose addresses can be found at global.penguinrandomhouse.com.

First published by Penguin Random House Australia Pty Ltd, 2017

1 3 5 7 9 10 8 6 4 2

Text copyright © Jo Sandhu, 2017

Cover and text design by Bruno Herfst © Penguin Random House Australia Pty Ltd
Cover illustration © Kim Van Deun, 2017
Typeset in Adobe caslon by Bruno Herfst, Penguin Random House Australia Pty Ltd
Colour separation by Splitting Image Colour Studio, Clayton, Victoria
Printed and bound in Australia by Griffin Press, an accredited ISO AS/NZS 14001
Environmental Management Systems printer

National Library of Australia Cataloguing-in-Publication data:

Sandhu, Jo, author
Tarin of the Mammoths: The Exile/Jo Sandhu

ISBN: 978 0 14 330937 6

A823.4

www.penguin.com.au

To Sarj, Chris and Alex –
with much love

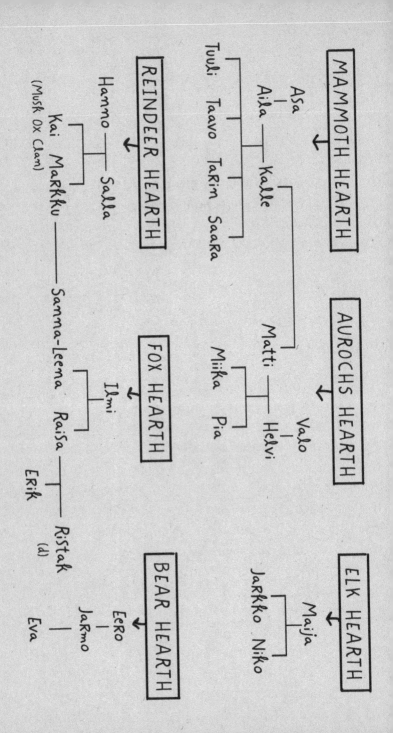

Prologue

The wind smells of snow.

I pull my hood forward and wriggle my frozen toes and frozen fingers. I hunch in the shelter of the rock cliff and look down towards the valley. It's the last mammoth hunt of the season, and below me, the hunters are moving into position.

I wave to my brother, Taavo, but he doesn't see me. It is his first hunt, and he grips his spear tightly and leans into the wind. A copse of sagebrush and stubby pine shelters him as he waits for the mammoths.

My breath steams the air around me. I'm glad I have my warm clothes. My hood is made of wolverine, with two flaps hanging down over my ears. My foot-coverings and leggings are made of rabbit skin, like my mittens. My mother made them for me, with the pelts my father trapped down by the river. My mother makes the best furs and leathers, and my father makes spears that are straight and strong. Sometimes he tips the ends with flakes of flint and bone. He made Taavo's spear especially for his first hunt, and carved it with symbols for good luck and good hunting.

'Will you carve a spear for me, Father?' I asked him, watching him rub the wood with sand to make it smooth.

'For you, little rabbit?' He laughed, his voice as big and deep as a bear's. 'For you I will carve a special digging stick, and you can help Old Mother gather her herbs and plants.'

But I don't want to help Old Mother gather the plants. I want to hunt mammoth and bison and reindeer. I want to have my own spear and tell my own stories. But it is hard for me to run and hunt with the other boys. I am not strong like them, and my leg twists beneath me when I run. Old Mother makes me medicine, to give strength to my limbs, and Old Father sings songs to the Spirits and asks my totem, my guide, to help me.

'Spirit of Owl,' he sings. 'Silent Wise One . . .'

But maybe my Owl guide cannot hear him, or doesn't want to help me, because my leg stays weak and sometimes I find it hard to breathe.

'Skinny rabbit,' my mother calls me, but she smiles when she does.

'Weak one,' the other boys say, and they turn away to talk of hunting and bravery.

My brother is the only one who calls me by name, who stands by me.

'Tarin,' he says, 'when we are men, we will hunt together. You and I.'

But now he is hunting mammoth, and I am alone on a rock shelf above him, watching.

The wind has changed direction, bringing with it the deep rumbling boom of the mammoth herd. It thrills my heart. The ground trembles and I know they are getting close. Our runners have been out since first light, to find the mighty herd. An Old Mother is leading her tribe away from the heavy snowfalls in the forests and mountains and towards the open plains and their winter grounds, far away. It is the last herd to make the journey before Kaamos, and they will reach the grasslands as the world darkens and the Ice Mother covers the land in snow.

I lean forward to catch sight of the herd as they come closer. Slowly I edge further down the rocks. A few stray stones scrape under my foot and roll down into the canyon. The hunters all turn their faces towards me. Angry faces. But they say nothing, because the herd has paused by the entrance to the canyon. The Old Mother, their leader, is wary . . . nervous. She moves her great body from side to side, tasting the air, her dark-brown fur swaying with the motion.

My feet and my fingers feel numb, and I shift to try and ease the cramping pain in my poor leg. But it is a mistake. The loose rock beneath my feet gives way, and suddenly I am falling, the thunder of crashing rocks echoing around the canyon.

The Old Mother lifts her trunk and trumpets a warning. My ears ring with the sound. All around me is chaos, and still I fall towards the floor of the canyon, the cascading rocks shredding the skin from my hands as I try to stop.

The herd is stampeding away from the carefully laid trap. The hunters are shouting, running forward with flaming torches and spears, trying desperately to turn the frightened animals back. If they do, I will be crushed. But if they fail, we will have no meat to see us through the long, dark winter ahead.

With a rush, I land hard on the rocky floor. My head smashes into the rocks. Blood stings my eyes. I want to cry out, but my chest hurts and I cannot draw enough breath into my body. Like a frightened animal, I huddle in the shadow of the rocks, whimpering, unable to move.

A young bull thunders towards me, his new tusks already lethal weapons. I imagine them ripping open my stomach. My mouth and my eyes are full of dust and blood, but I can feel the ground shake as he charges.

I hear a shout and a spear rushes towards the young bull, only to shatter on the rocks beside me. It is my brother's spear. I can see the carving of his totem, the mighty bison, on its broken shaft. It is not lucky for him today.

But it is enough to startle the bull. He turns and runs, following his mother's frantic cries. The hunters try to follow them, but it is already too late – the herd have fled the canyon.

I wipe the dust from my eyes and look up. A tangle of shaggy brown fur sways above me, so close I could reach out and touch it. The Old Mother is watching me. I push myself to my feet and I see her high domed head and deep liquid eyes. Her tusks curve proudly, but they are pitted and aged and the right is broken at the tip. She reaches out with her trunk and touches my head with a gentle caress. Her breath is warm against my face.

I reach my hand towards her, and my fingertips brush her fur. Then she turns silently and is gone.

I am left alone on the canyon floor, the angry, frightened hunters of my clan running towards me.

The Council
Meeting

Tarin huddled in the darkened corner of the earth-lodge and watched as the flames danced to the beating drums. The rhythm was urgent . . . angry. The hollow sound of bone hitting bone echoed in his skull, making it ache. Normally, he enjoyed hearing the drums. In their rhythms and changing tones he heard stories of bountiful hunts and acts of great bravery. But tonight was different. Tonight, each beat of the mammoth skull drum was like a cold flint blade twisting deep into his stomach.

He plucked restlessly at the soft rabbit-skin bandages binding his hands and looked around the earth-lodge. Bison and reindeer hides covered the floor. Interlaced bones of mammoth and deer rose in a dome above him, glowing pale in the dim light. A spiral of smoke floated upwards, and Tarin wished that he, too, could float away.

His gaze dropped back to the fire and he studied the faces of the Mammoth Clan huddled around its warmth. Everyone was there, the young and the old, from the six hearths of the clan: Mammoth – his own hearth, Aurochs, Reindeer, Elk, Fox and Bear. Directly across from Tarin stood stern-faced Hanno, small rounded Salla and Markku of Reindeer Hearth. Next to them was frail old Eero of Bear Hearth, nodding his head in time with the drums. The youngest children huddled beside him like a pack of small wolf cubs.

'Tarin? Are you warm enough? Come closer to the fire.' Sanna-Leena of Reindeer Hearth moved to make room for him. She held her new baby close to her chest and crooned softly.

She looks worried, Tarin thought. They all look worried.

He closed his eyes, blocking out the fear on their faces. But he couldn't block the angry murmurings and muffled whispers.

'Two hunts in a row have failed . . .'

'We cannot survive the Long Dark this way . . .'

'But I saw the She-mammoth touch him . . .'

The drumbeat rose, drowning the heated voices. It was Miika and Jarkko on the drums tonight. Their muscles strained as they pounded the bones. Sweat ran down their faces, but in his shadowy corner Tarin shivered. Already the seasons were changing. The cold winds blew and the last seed heads hung grimly to the dry grasses of the plains. To the south, the red and gold leaves of autumn were falling to the ground. The days were shorter now, the nights longer. Soon it would be *Kaamos*, the time of the Long Dark, and without their stores of rich mammoth meat, winter would be a hard season for Mammoth Clan.

'The boy is bad luck!'

The drums stopped abruptly, and the woman's voice carried clearly. From across the fire, Tarin felt the cold, spiteful glare of Maija of Elk Hearth. Her face was pinched and angry, her arms folded across her chest.

Tarin dropped his eyes and tried to slide further into the shadows. He pulled at the bandage around his head. It felt too tight.

'Old Mother, I want to go.'

'Stop that.' Asa, Old Mother, who shared his hearth, slapped his hand away. Deepset grey eyes glared at him fiercely. 'And drink this.' Tarin took the small bone cup from her and choked as the hot liquid burned his throat. He tasted bitter willowbark and meadow sage. 'Tie your hair back and do not hide like a coward.' She threw a strip of leather into his lap. Then her gaze softened and she clicked her tongue. 'Little rabbit, you must be brave.'

'I . . . I don't think I can,' Tarin whispered. His fingers shook as he wrapped the thong around his hair.

'Shh, courage, little one.' She gripped Tarin's shoulder and forced him to sit tall. Her gnarled fingers dug deep into his flesh. Tarin kept his eyes down and stared at the flames. He wanted to look for his mother, but he didn't want her to see the fear in his eyes.

'Weakling child,' Maija said. 'He will never be the man Kalle is.'

Tarin clenched his teeth. All his life he had heard people mutter and wonder aloud: How could Kalle and Aila, the two strong leaders of Mammoth Clan, have such a weak, sickly son? It must be the bad Spirits . . .

'People of the Mammoth Clan.' A deep voice filled the lodge, and all eyes turned to their leader. Kalle looked around the clan with a stern gaze. His eyes flickered briefly over his son, and Tarin winced at the pain he saw there.

'We welcome the Spirits here tonight, and ask for their protection and guidance.' Kalle raised his hands in the air and began a deep, rumbling chant. Slowly the drums joined in, and then the rest of the clan. They lifted their hands to the sky and beseeched the Spirits to look with favour upon the Clan of the Mammoths.

But Tarin didn't feel like singing tonight. He hung his head miserably and waited in the shadows. Maija was right.

He would never be the man his father was.

Once, Kalle had faced a full-grown cave bear. Tarin had heard the story many times: how his father laughed in the face of death, armed only with a small flint knife. Now, he wore the cave bear's teeth and claws around his neck. A cloak of mammoth fur hung from his shoulders, just brushing the ground. Two boar tusks adorned his fur headpiece, and by his side hung the ceremonial clan knife, a narrow flint blade nestled in a pouch of bison leather.

The chant changed. Now it was a song of hunting and bravery. The men's voices dropped as the women's took over. Tarin heard his mother's voice rise above the rest. Her heavy necklet of amber and bone shone in the flickering firelight. Carved ivory beads and shells entwined through her hair and she, too, carried a knife at her waist. But Tarin also saw the dark shadows beneath her eyes and the way her fingers twisted in the long mammoth fur that fringed her buckskin tunic.

The songs were short tonight. The drums stilled. The silence deepened. Tarin felt cold, although the fire and the press of bodies warmed the air inside the earth-lodge. Old Mother gripped his wrist, and her bony fingers felt like claws. But there was strength there, too. It was the strength that ran in the blood of the Mammutti. It was the strength that had always brought them through the harsh winters of this unforgiving land. But maybe this time – Tarin shivered and turned his hand to clasp Asa's – maybe this time it would not be enough.

Maybe this time, our clan will not survive . . .

Valo, Spirit Keeper of Mammoth Clan, and Old Father to them all, stepped forward. He wore a crown of deer antlers upon his head and his face was marked with the sacred red ochre. He carried a staff made from the straightened tusk of a mammoth, and decorated with feathers and carved bone.

Old Father closed his eyes and waved his hands over the flames. Sweat ran down his face and fell hissing onto the rocks piled around the fire pit. With a sudden movement, he plunged his hand into a small leather pouch at his waist and flung a handful of dried herbs over the flames.

The clan gasped and cried out as the flames leapt upwards, the scorching heat forcing them back into the shadows.

Tarin's eyes stung as he picked out the strong, pungent scent of dried wormwood and pine. He tried not to cough, but his throat burned as smoke filled the lodge.

A small, sturdy figure wriggled through the crowd and sat next to him. His sister's hand crept into his and she leaned her head on his arm. 'It smells,' Saara said, wrinkling her nose.

Old Mother shushed them both. Old Father was telling

a story, his voice washing over the clan, soothing their fears and comforting them. He was telling the story of how the fearsome Ice Mother was jealous of her sister, the gentle Earth Mother, and each winter they fought a terrible battle. Tarin had heard the story many times. It was how Old Father began each clan meeting, because it was the story of their land.

'And the gentle Earth Mother trembled, and the light left the world. And into the Long Dark came the Ice Mother, and she covered the land in her rivers of ice and laughed as the people wept. But the Earth Mother never gave up. Each year she fought the Ice Mother, pushing back the darkness, bringing life once more to the land.' Old Father's voice faded away and the children sighed in enjoyment.

'But sometimes,' Old Father continued, 'we forget to thank the Earth Mother for her goodness. Sometimes, she chooses to withhold her light, her bounty, from us. Two hunts have failed.' His wavering voice filled the silent lodge. 'The Earth Mother has turned her face from us . . . and we are left alone.'

'The Earth Mother has forsaken us. That boy has brought us misfortune,' Maija cried, pointing an accusing finger at Tarin.

'No, we do not believe that.' Jarkko stepped in front of his mother and gave her a stern look. 'I speak for Elk

16

Hearth, and I say the boy is not at fault . . .'

'But he did frighten the mammoths,' said a younger voice, Miika of Aurochs Hearth. He folded his arms across his chest and glared at Tarin. 'Taavo and I were nearly injured.'

'And what were you and Taavo doing in the canyon?' Matti, his father, frowned at him. 'I told you to wait and be ready to light the torches.'

'There would have been no need for torches if Tarin hadn't frightened the mammoths.'

'He didn't mean to!' Saara jumped up and confronted the taller boy.

'That's right,' said Raisa of Fox Hearth, her voice gentle. 'It was an accident. A terrible accident.'

'There have been too many hunting accidents lately,' Maija snapped.

Jarmo of Bear Hearth growled. 'Are you now blaming the boy for Ristak's death?'

Maija shrugged and lifted her hands. Bone bracelets on her wrists clinked together.

'But Ristak was gored by a bison. How could Tarin be held responsible?' Raisa's voice broke, and tears ran down her face. 'Ristak was a brave hunter . . . and I miss him. I miss him every day. But Tarin was not there.'

'Two spoiled hunts, and one of our strong hunters dead. He is bad luck.' Maija scowled.

17

The lodge erupted. Angry voices shouted, one on top of the other.

'You will not blame my son for this misfortune, Maija,' Aila said.

'Then who should we blame? That was our last chance to hunt the mammoth before Winter, and now we will all starve.'

'We will not starve.' Aila's voice was sharp. She placed an arm around the weeping Raisa.

'Then what are we going to do?'

Voices rose . . . anxious . . . worried. Tarin shook his head. He didn't like this meeting. It was too angry, and too serious. A hard shoulder jostled him, breaking his train of thought.

'Taavo, where have you been?' Tarin whispered as his brother threw himself to the floor and sat glaring at the fire.

'What do you care?' Taavo snarled. 'You ruined the hunt. My first hunt. It was to be my Manhood hunt.' He turned angrily from Tarin and refused to look at him.

'Enough!' bellowed Kalle. His huge voice cut through the arguments. Silence fell on the lodge. 'I will speak.' Tarin felt his face turn red and he lowered his eyes. His father continued. 'We will still have a First Hunt for Taavo.'

'But what will we hunt?' Taavo's voice rose in frustration. 'The mammoths have gone. The bison are far to the south. I will not hunt rabbits for my Manhood hunt!'

'I said *enough*!' Kalle's eyes flashed in anger at his oldest son. 'I have not finished.' He waited until the only sounds in the lodge were the crackling fire and the creaking of the bones as the wind tried to find gaps in the lodge walls. Tarin once believed that when the bones howled and groaned, it was their ancestor Spirits come to talk to them.

'We are the Mammutti – hunters of the great mammoths. We are not a pack of cave hyenas that squabble and fight over carrion.' The clan shuffled their feet and looked down. 'And yet, we must ask ourselves – have we offended the Earth Mother? Why has she chosen to withhold her bounty from us?'

'We have taken the goodness of the Earth Mother for granted,' said Old Father. He pounded his heavy bone staff into the ground. An owl feather came loose from its leather tie and floated free. It landed on the ground next to Tarin's foot. 'Each season, she fills our bellies with grains from the fields, herbs from the meadows and fish from the rivers. From the plains, she gives to us her mightiest gifts – mammoth, bison and aurochs. She gives these gifts so that we may live. But we have forgotten this. We take, and we do not give.'

Kalle nodded, his face grim. 'The boy, Tarin, will stand.'

Tarin wrenched his eyes away from the owl feather and Old Mother pulled him to his feet. His heart pounded. His legs were made of water. He wanted to cling to Old Mother, to clutch hold of her hand and never let go, but she prised her fingers from his grip. Tarin wiped his hands down his leggings and swallowed hard. He forced himself to lift his chin and stand before the clan. He couldn't bring himself to look Kalle in the eye. Instead, he focused on his father's right shoulder.

'Tarin, by your actions, you endangered not only yourself, but also the hunters of your clan.'

'I . . . I know.' Tarin knew his reply sounded small and weak.

'Hunts have failed before, and will fail again. But to survive, the clan must work together as one.'

'I know . . . and . . . I'm truly sorry.' Tarin raised his eyes to his father's, and then quickly dropped them again. Kalle studied his son. The silence stretched. The clan moved restlessly, waiting for their leader to speak. A baby woke, looking for food, and was quickly hushed.

Kalle sighed. 'I will speak with the elders of each Hearth family,' he said. 'Before making my decision.' He turned away from Tarin. 'Tuuli, take the children and give them food. You will be called when a decision is made.'

A blast of cold air pushed Tarin backwards as he followed his eldest sister from the earth-lodge. He shook her arm urgently.

'Tuuli, what is going to happen?'

'I don't know, Tarin.' Tuuli closed her eyes and sighed. Tarin frowned. She looked tired. She and the other young clan women had trekked far that day, digging sedge roots along the riverbank where the soil was still soft, and scraping reindeer moss off the rocks.

'Come on, you lot.' Tuuli herded the younger children – Saara, Eva, Erik and Niko – towards Reindeer Lodge, where Salla had prepared food for them. 'I'm going to tell you a story.'

'But it's warmer in Mammoth Lodge,' said Niko, looking back. 'Why can't we stay there?'

'Because we can't,' said Tuuli. She held open the flap of mammoth hide and pushed Niko forward into the lodge. The welcoming smell of simmering stew filled their nostrils.

'Because the grown-ups are talking about Tarin,' said Saara. 'Isn't that right, Tuuli?' She looked at her older sister for confirmation.

'I'm sure they're talking about a lot of things . . .'

'I think they should banish Tarin,' said Erik. 'He ruined the hunt.'

Tarin scowled and crouched miserably on the floor.

'Don't say that about my brother.' Saara pushed the older boy.

'Stop it, both of you,' said Tuuli, rubbing her forehead.

She added shaved slivers of bone to the fire and Tarin, shivering, held his hands towards it. 'Saara, pass me those plates. See how they're made of bone? I'm going to tell you a story of a place where the plates are made from wood. Deep in the forest, the Metsamaa clans live . . .'

'Where's Taavo?' Erik asked. 'And Miika and Pia?'

'They said they didn't want to eat with a weakling coward,' said Niko. 'I wanted to go with them, too . . .'

'I'm not a coward,' Tarin growled.

'Yes, you are,' said Niko. 'Miika says that's why you don't hunt. Because you're scared.'

'I am not!' Tarin jumped to his feet. His hands clenched into fists.

'Miika says you will never be a hunter like us, and you should just leave.' Niko shovelled a scoop of stew into his mouth and chewed thoughtfully.

'Then Tarin will just find another clan to live with.' Saara scowled at him.

'What other clan? Miika says Tarin is bad luck, and if he can't hunt, what use is he to anyone?'

'That's not a nice thing to say, Niko,' said Tuuli. 'And if you can't think of something nice to say, you can just sit there and keep quiet.'

Niko shrugged and lifted his bowl to his lips, draining the rest of his food. 'It's what everyone says,' he muttered.

'My mother says if Tarin isn't banished, maybe we'll leave and find another clan. Maybe we'll live with Saiga Clan or Bison Clan.'

'Maija said that?' Tuuli sounded surprised, then she shook her head. 'Winter is nearly here. You can't leave until Summer.'

Tarin turned his back on Niko and Erik. Tuuli offered him a plate.

'I'm not hungry,' he mumbled.

'You should eat.' His sister sat down next to him. She glanced at the other children and lowered her voice. 'Tarin? Why did you go to the canyon? You know you weren't supposed to be there.'

'I . . . don't know.' Tarin's voice shook and he hunched his shoulders angrily. 'I just did.'

'Is it . . .' Tuuli stopped and bit her lip. She laid a hand on Tarin's shoulder, but he flinched, and she moved it away. 'Your weaknesses mean nothing to us, Tarin. You are so loved. It doesn't matter that you can't hunt.'

'I don't want to be pitied, Tuuli. I don't want to be "loved". I want to be a hunter. I want . . .' Tarin's voice stuck in his throat and he jumped to his feet. He had to get out of there, away from Tuuli's pitying looks and Niko's contempt. He pushed his way past them and out into the cold night air. It froze his lungs as he drew in a deep breath. The night was clear, and a couple of early stars twinkled above him. A bright full moon hung low over the steppes, turning everything to silver. He heard soft footsteps approach and Tuuli appeared beside him.

'Niko's right,' said Tarin. 'No other clan would have me.'

'You don't need another clan, Tarin. You belong here.'

'It doesn't feel like it.' Tarin shrugged. As though from a great distance, he heard the sound of the drums. A tremor shook his thin body. 'They've made their decision.'

'They won't banish you, Tarin. They won't.' But Tuuli's voice was fearful. Brother and sister both looked bleakly at Mammoth Lodge. A tall figure stepped from the lodge and the drums became momentarily louder. Jarkko walked towards them with slow, steady steps.

'It is time, little rabbit.' He squeezed Tarin's shoulder. Tarin felt the warmth of his grip through his tunic. 'You need to come with me.'

Tarin nodded. He felt numb. There was nothing he could do, except turn and follow Jarkko back to Mammoth Lodge.

Fever

Night was drawing in. Kaija cast a quick glance over her shoulder. The noises of the forest unsettled her. Snow was already falling and her breath steamed the chilly air as she placed the bones in the proper position. She struggled to balance the two crossed deer legs, and she pulled her mittens off impatiently with her teeth. The cold seeped into her fingers, numbing them.

She sat back on her haunches and studied the bones. They gleamed white in the moonlight. The empty eye sockets of the bear's skull stared sightlessly at her. She shivered and pulled her fur around her shoulders. The bones were a warning to travellers. A warning of sickness . . . of danger. It would have to do.

She rubbed her face and sighed deeply. She was so tired. A rustle of leaves, the crunch of running feet on newly fallen snow – the sounds echoed loudly in the silent forest.

An owl hooted quietly and rose into the air like mist.

'Kaija!'

She rose to her feet at the sound of her brother's voice. 'Luuka, what is it?'

Luuka bent over to catch his breath and grasped her arm. She felt his fingers dig into her.

'You have to come. It's Retu.'

Fear gripped her heart. Like the ice of the long, dark winter.

'No . . .' The word was a moan, captured by the night wind and carried away. 'Not Retu.' Her hand brushed her forehead. It felt clammy. She stared at the beads of sweat glistening on her fingertips.

'Kaija? You too?' Luuka turned her to study her face. He looked at her with anxious eyes.

'No.' She shook her head and tried to move away from him. 'I ran to place the bones. That's all.'

He nodded, but still the worried look remained.

They didn't speak as they ran back to the cave. Their pounding feet and the thudding of their hearts were the only noise in the forest. Kaija paused at the entrance to their cave. The fresh air had given her a reprieve from the stench of sickness and death, but it surrounded her again now. It was suffocating. She put her hand over her nostrils and tried not to breathe in.

Her eyes adjusted to the flickering firelight, and she hurried to her mother's side. She lowered her head to avoid the ravaged faces, the red, anguished eyes, the empty stares of those who had already died. Her mother's back was bowed, her head hidden in her hands.

'Not the boy . . .' she wailed. 'Not my son. Don't take my son from me.'

Kaija drew in a ragged breath. She knelt by her mother and felt her brother's brow. It was too late. His thin body gleamed with sweat and weeping sores. His eyes stared sightlessly at the roof of the cave.

The Spirit Keeper loomed above them like a shadow. His face was covered in ash, his eyes ringed with red ochre. He rattled a staff of bleached bones over Retu and moaned. He brought his face close to Kaija and she smelled the sickness on his breath. His bloodshot eyes stared at her.

'It is a judgement,' he said, spraying his spittle.

Kaija recoiled. She grasped Luuka's hand and glared at the Spirit Keeper. 'How can a child's death be a judgement?'

The Spirit Keeper turned to the woman weeping over her son. 'It is a judgment against you, Senja. The healer who cannot heal.'

Kaija's mother moaned and covered her face. 'Nothing I do helps. Nothing.'

Kaija jumped to her feet. 'That's unfair. You are the Spirit

Keeper. Why don't you ask the Spirits for help?'

The Spirit Keeper snarled at her and rattled his bones before melting into the shadows.

Senja pulled her arm. 'Do not anger the Spirits further, Kaija. He may be our Spirit Keeper, but he is also a man in pain. He has lost his hearth-mate and his child to this plague.'

'We have all lost loved ones, mother,' Luuka said. He leant forward and closed Retu's sightless eyes.

Senja's head drooped, as though she would sleep. Kaija hissed and took her mother's face between her hands, looking deep into her glazed eyes. 'Mother! You've taken the herbs again!'

Senja sighed deeply and brought her focus back to her daughter. 'I know you don't like me to take them, Kaija.'

'It's so dangerous!'

'But they help me to see things I couldn't see otherwise. They help me heal people. I see their sickness in my dreams, and I see the bad Spirits around them.'

'What do you see now, mother?' Kaija replied, her voice low and sad. Senja stared at Retu's tiny body and shuddered.

'I see a blackness upon this clan,' she whispered. 'I see the faceless grey Spirits come to take us all.'

'Mother! Stop it.' Kaija grabbed her arms and shook her, but her mother didn't listen to her.

'I cannot fight against these Spirits, Kaija. They are too strong.' Her eyes were once more unfocused, large and staring. Her hand crept to her throat as though she couldn't breathe. 'But in my dreams, I have seen the mammoths ...'

Kaija scrubbed at the tears on her cheeks. 'I don't understand.' Her mother's dreams never made sense.

'I have seen them, moving always northward, towards the place where the Great Mother dances in the sky.' She closed her eyes and swayed. 'It must mean something, Kaija. It must. Why else would I dream of them, night after night? And why is there always the one small one, lagging behind? His leg is hurt, and his heart is heavy. He walks in danger ...'

Luuka passed her a cup of water. 'Drink,' he said firmly. Then he refilled the cup and gave it to Kaija. 'When is the last time any of us has eaten? It is no wonder our thoughts are strange.'

Slowly, Senja's breathing steadied, and the glazed look faded from her eyes.

Kaija took her mother's hands in hers. They were cool to touch and soft from the beaver fat ointments she used in her healing. 'Mother, this sickness, is there no end to it?' How many days had passed, Kaija wondered, since the first member of her clan had fallen sick. Ten? Twenty? The first to die was old Lia, which surprised no one, but then another fell sick, and another. First, with fever and aching bones. Then the coughing started and their necks hurt to touch. Kaija's hand rested on her throat and she swallowed hard. She had brewed teas and bathed open wounds. She had held frail bodies when they struggled to breathe, and sung to them as the light left their eyes and their spirits left them. How many more? her heart cried. How many more would die?

'There is no end,' Senja said, her voice weary. She glanced around the cave and beckoned them closer. 'That's why you have to flee, my children.'

'No,' Kaija said.

'Mother, we can't just leave you,' Luuka said. He knelt down beside her and took one of her hands.

'You can. You must.' Their mother squeezed their hands then pushed them away. 'But you must be quick. If you stay here . . . If you should get sick . . .' Her voice failed. 'Luuka, take your sister. Make her go. Make for Beaver Clan. They will help you. But you have to go now, before anyone sees you. They will try and stop you.'

'I won't leave you –' Kaija pulled against Luuka's hand.

'You must, child. It is dangerous for you here.'

'Then we will all go. You and me and Luuka –'

'Child, it is too late. I already have the sickness in me. I can feel it.'

'No!' Kaija reached for her mother, but Luuka pulled her

to her feet and shook her shoulders.

'Mother is right. This sickness, whatever it is, is killing us all. I don't mind for me, if it is my time to journey to the Spirit World, but it is not your time, Kaija. I know that.'

'How can you know? I can stay and help nurse them.'

'No.' Senja bent low over Retu so her face couldn't be seen. She spoke in a low voice. 'I've seen the men look this way, and whisper amongst themselves. You have to run. Now.'

'At least let us bury Retu first.' Kaija touched the small boy's hair. 'Let us rub the red ochre on him and sing to him, so he can find his way home to the Spirit World.'

'I will do that. Trust me,' said Senja.

Kaija couldn't bring herself to look at her mother. Instead, she stared at the small ring of stones circling their fire pit.

'Luuka, do you remember the day you and Retu collected those stones, down near the river? How proud he was to be out with his big brother.' Kaija's voice wavered.

Luuka smiled sadly. 'There were so many trout, they were jumping out of the water. I remember. It took us days to dry the fillets.'

'River Clan was happy then.' Kaija shook her head and dragged her thoughts back to the present. Those days were gone, and Retu would never again fish with his brother and he would never again sit in his sister's lap and sing with her.

'Kaija, I know you don't believe in my dreams, but they must have some meaning,' Senja said. 'Find the mammoths. They can help us.' Then she frowned. 'But they also need your help. I feel that in my bones. The little one especially.'

'Girl!' A voice called from across the cave. 'I need water.'

Kaija wiped her eyes. 'Mother, we will talk about this further.'

She grabbed a water flask and hurried to the woman beckoning her.

'Asha, be comfortable. Here is water.' She held the flask to the sick woman's lips and helped her to drink. Asha groaned. Her face was flushed and hollow.

'It hurts to breathe,' she said, her chest labouring to rise and fall. Kaija wet a soft rabbit skin and wiped her face. She murmured soothing words. 'I want an end to this.' Asha tried to grip Kaija's hand, but she had no strength in her wasted muscles. 'Tell Senja to make the tea. I want to sleep with the Spirits.'

'Asha, do not give in,' Kaija said.

'Easy for you to say, girl. You are not the one who is in pain. You do not struggle for every breath. You and your brother.' She lay back in exhaustion and studied Kaija carefully from half-closed eyes. 'They say you have special medicine. That your mother has kept special herbs just for her children.'

'She would never do that.' Kaija pushed Asha's hand away. 'And my little brother has just died. Why would my mother let her son die if she had special herbs?'

Asha sniffed and struggled with another breath. 'They say you have bad magic in you. Two born together should not have lived, but your mother used secret ways to keep you alive. Perhaps even now that special magic is still in your bones.'

'You do not know what you are saying, Asha.' She tried to speak soothingly.

'Kaija.' Luuka crossed the cave toward her. 'Mother says she needs more water. We have to go and fill the flasks at the river.'

'Now?' Kaija stumbled to her feet. She was upset not only by Asha's pain, but by her words. 'It is so late.'

Asha drew a painful breath and snorted. It almost sounded like a laugh. 'Go with your brother, girl. Run while you can.'

'I don't understand what you mean –' Kaija started to say, but Luuka grabbed her wrist so tightly it made her gasp.

'It means, girl, you should leave, before they take you and grind your bones to get that special magic.'

'They wouldn't!' Kaija went pale.

'They would.' Asha coughed and sputtered. The foam around her mouth was tinted red. 'Run while you can.'

Kaija stared at her in horror. 'I can't just leave. I have to help my mother.' She tried to move away, but Luuka stopped her. He brought his mouth close to her ear.

'We are in danger, Kaija. Do what our mother asks. She will follow us to Beaver Clan.'

Kaija strained against his hold.

'No, don't go to her. Don't argue. Just this once,' he pleaded.

Kaija shivered. From the corner of her eye, she was suddenly aware of the men casting glances their way. They had been surly and unhelpful all day – first, when she asked them to give water to the sick, and again when she needed them to help lift the bodies. Now they stood in a group at the mouth of the cave, muttering together.

She rubbed her arms, suddenly cold. 'They may not let us past.' She wet her lips. They felt dry and cracked.

'Water!' Asha called out suddenly. 'Stupid, useless girl! You have spilled all the water!'

'Kaija! Luuka! I need you to get more water,' their mother called from the other side of the cave.

With fumbling hands, Kaija grabbed the water bag. She dared not look at her mother. She dared not look at Retu's tiny body lying cold and alone in their corner of the cave. She made herself move slowly towards the cave entrance on legs that felt weak and unfamiliar.

Behind her, Luuka's voice was firm as he spoke to the men. 'We are filling the flasks. We need more water.'

A man grunted and let them pass, out into the cold darkness. Kaija drew in a sharp breath and the frosty air pierced her chest. She started to shake, but Luuka put an arm around her and urged her onwards. Tears flowed down her cheeks, but there was no time to mourn now. Silently, brother and sister disappeared into the shadowy forest, and away from their home.

At first they kept to the river. The paths here were familiar to them both, leading to all their favourite fishing holes. They ran silently, fearfully. Luuka led the way, threading amongst the rocks and needing very little light to find his way. Behind him, Kaija stumbled, and he slowed his pace. A turned ankle or broken bone now would be a disaster.

'Can you go on?' Luuka asked.

She nodded. She knew she must look frightened and pale in the moonlight, but she tried to be brave. 'We brought nothing with us. How will we survive until Beaver Clan?'

Luuka rubbed his face. 'Up ahead there is a small cave I use when fishing. I leave supplies there.'

'So you don't have to answer questions when you slip out at night-time?'

'Mother worries too much,' he said, and shrugged. Then his eyes gleamed. 'The best fishing is at night.'

'The best sleeping is at night,' Kaija said, and pushed him onwards.

Minutes later they found the cave and Luuka's small bundle of supplies.

'I once caught a trout here, as big as that new baby of Mara's,' he said, smiling at the memory, but then his smile dimmed and the light left his eyes. Mara and her baby had died only yesterday. He rubbed his nose and sounded gruff. 'It broke my best gorge.' He unwound the leather tie from his bag and tipped it out.

'There's not much here.' Kaija chewed her lip. A flint blade; some fire-making tools – a small wooden platform and a stick; an assortment of bone and wooden gorges attached to thin ropes of braided willow; a few strips of dried fish and elm seeds.

'It's all we have,' said Luuka. 'If we had stopped to pack anything else, we would have been caught.'

'I haven't eaten today,' Kaija said, her voice wobbling. 'I was looking after Retu, and everyone kept calling me.' She scrubbed at her face to stop the tears from falling. 'He was so small.'

'Don't think of him.' Luuka's voice was sharp. 'We can think of Retu and Mother later. When we're safe.'

He passed her a strip of fish and took one himself, but then he hesitated. 'Kaija?' When he didn't continue, Kaija turned to look at him. He was turning the fish over in his hands and frowning. 'Do you think it was my fish that made the clan sick?'

'No, of course not,' Kaija said. 'Why would you think that?'

He shrugged. 'It's just that . . . the first one to fall ill was that trader from upriver. You remember? He traded us the reindeer meat for our salmon. I added in some grayling because he showed me how to carve a gorge from the reindeer antler.'

'So?'

'So . . . what if it was the grayling? We all ate it that night, and the next day he was sick.'

Kaija sat on her haunches and stared at her brother. His eyes were shadowed with tiredness. 'But it was the bad Spirits that made us sick,' she said. 'The Spirit Keeper said so.'

'But what if he is wrong?' Luuka jumped up. 'We were all fine, until that night.'

Kaija frowned. 'We ate the fish, and the reindeer, and some of those little burdock roots we had in storage. And late hazelnuts. But if it was the food, Mother would have known. She tried everything – yarrow and horsetail and

37

even wolf moss.' She shook her head. 'No, it wasn't the food. I still think it was the Spirits.'

'But why would the Spirits want to do that to us?' Luuka said. 'So many have died. So many good people . . . and the children . . .'

'I know, but what else could it be?' Kaija stared at the strip of fish. 'A moment ago you told me not to think of Retu. Now, I'm telling you. Don't think of any of them. We can't help them anymore, and I'm too hungry to argue with you.' She stuffed the dried fish into her mouth and chewed.

Luuka shrugged and copied her. 'This is trout, anyway.' He packed the rest of the supplies back into the bag. 'We leave the river here. The path is too dangerous in the dark. A little further then we can sleep until first light.' He paused and looked around the familiar surroundings. 'I shall miss this river,' he said. He kicked at some old dry fish scales that glowed silver in the moonlight. 'There's the rock I used to scrape the scales off my catch. And I still have willow traps floating somewhere out there in the darkness.' He picked up a smooth, grey stone and tossed it into the water. 'It was a good fishing hole.' He reached his hand down to his sister and pulled her to her feet.

'Farewell, Retu. Walk brave with the Spirits, little brother,' he whispered, and they turned and left the camp.

A Decision
is Made

Tarin forced himself to keep walking, one step after another, with feet as heavy as rocks.

'Stand tall, Tarin,' Jarkko said. 'Show them that you are a man.'

'But I'm not.' Tarin's voice was a broken whisper.

They had come to the entrance of the earth-lodge and Tarin stopped. The sound of voices filtered out. He wished he could hear what they were saying, but the bone and earth walls were too thick. The mammoth tusks framing the entrance were white in the moonlight and a stiff breeze shook the heavy mammoth hide door. Jarkko stamped his feet and blew on his hands while Tarin stood motionless.

'We have to go in, Tarin.' Jarkko grasped Tarin's shoulders and squatted down, so they were looking straight at one another. Tarin saw sorrow and determination in the man's warm hazel eyes. He wondered what Jarkko saw in his eyes. Probably fear, he thought. Grey fear, like the mist that creeps across the landscape and freezes everything in its path.

Jarkko shook him gently and smiled. 'I saw the She-mammoth. I saw her choose you. You are a man, but you have to believe that yourself. Don't believe what others say.'

Tarin opened his mouth to speak, but Jarkko was already pushing aside the door and stepping down into the earth-lodge. Tarin felt a wave of warm air beckon him inside, and he moved forward. He stumbled slightly on the step down into the rounded chamber and blinked as his eyes adjusted to the firelight. Sombre faces circled the fire. All the elders of the Hearths were here.

Helvi moved forward and took Tarin by the hands. 'Your hands are like ice, child.' She rubbed his frozen skin and drew him towards the fire.

Tarin searched the shadows for his mother. His eyes passed over gruff Matti, stroking his long beard, and tiny Ilmi with her wrinkled face and toothless smile. Ilmi's black eyes twinkled in the firelight and Tarin thought she winked at him. He glanced quickly to her left. Scowling, hard-faced Maija. Tarin dropped his eyes and studied the floor. He felt it was safer. The owl feather was still there, caught on a rock that circled the fire pit.

A cold breeze entered the lodge and all eyes turned towards the door. Miika and Taavo stepped through, then Pia and Erik. Tuuli and the younger children followed after them. Tarin's heart sank. If he were to be banished, he would prefer to hear it without the laughing jeers of the other children. He swallowed hard and turned to face his father.

Kalle frowned at the clan's younger members as they pushed into the circle around the fire, but he waited until they were settled before raising his hands for silence.

'Boy, go forward.' Old Mother poked Tarin in the back. He shuffled forward a step, noticing as he did that the owl feather had now attached itself to his boot. It was caught in a long strand of mammoth wool. 'Head up,' Old Mother hissed, but Tarin felt as though his head was a lump of rock that wouldn't move.

Kalle raised his voice and spoke to the clan. 'The leaders of each Hearth have offered their advice and I have listened.' His eyes rested thoughtfully on Maija. 'I have listened to all who chose to voice their opinions.' He reached for the ceremonial mammoth staff and banged it three times into the ground. 'And I have made my decision. We have a hard season ahead of us . . .' He paused and waited for stray whispers to cease and every member of Mammoth Clan to turn their eyes towards him. Every member except Tarin, who stood with his head down and his eyes focused on his boots. 'Tarin, son of Mammoth Clan, we will not banish you, for to do so would surely mean your death ...'

He wasn't banished ... Tarin's knees wobbled.

'But we declare you *Haamu*.' Kalle held his staff over his head and drove it into the earthen floor. 'You shall speak to no one ...' Again the staff shook the lodge. 'And take only what food and water is left when we have eaten, until three times the full moon lights the night sky. In this way, you shall be exiled from your Hearth and from your Clan, but you will live. So have I, Kalle of Mammoth Hearth, Leader of Mammoth Clan, spoken.'

Haamu! Tarin drew a deep breath and sank to the floor as his legs collapsed beneath him. He pressed his palms to his eyes before the clan could see the tears threatening to run down his cheeks. He heard Maija's snort of disgust, voices muttering, angry and unsettled. Matti cleared his throat and spat, the wad of phlegm landing close to Tarin's boot. Tuuli clasped Tarin's wrists and sat down next to him, colour returning to her pale face.

'*Haamu*,' she whispered. 'It is not so bad.'

I'm not banished. I'm not banished! For three Moons he would live as an Exile amongst his clan, but he would survive. He raised his eyes to his father's face, and the relief that filled his heart faltered. His father's eyes were filled with so much pain . . . so much shame. Tarin hung his head.

'But taking food from one skinny child will not feed us all Winter,' Markku said with a growl. He put one arm around Sanna-Leena and the other rested on their baby.

Voices filled with anger and fear lapped one over the other, talking, crying, shouting. Kalle raised his hands for quiet, and slowly the mutter of voices subsided.

It's only my father that stops us from tearing at each other's throats like a pack of wolves, Tarin thought, and he shuddered, suddenly afraid for Mammoth Clan.

Kalle raised his voice so all would hear. 'That is why you will all be quiet and listen to Valo, Spirit Keeper.'

Valo stood and raised his hands in the air. He flung another handful of herbs into the fire and flames flared upwards to touch the bones above.

'What the Mother has given us, she can also withhold,' said Old Father. 'We have forgotten this. I have talked with the Spirits. With Spirit of Mammoth, our clan totem, and with Spirit of Bear, my own totem.' He looked around the circle of faces with hooded eyes and his gaze rested longest on Tarin. His lips thinned. His nostrils flared. 'They have told me that the great Earth Mother has not forsaken her children, but She is afraid we have forgotten her . . .'

'But that's not true,' Salla gasped. 'I thank Her every day!'

'It is not enough!' Old Father's voice rose. He shook his staff fiercely. 'If we do not want the Great Mother to forsake us – we must act now! The Spirits have told me we must send an Offering to the Earth Mother, to show Her the People of the Mammoth have not forgotten Her!'

The clan stared at each other, their minds slowly turning from fear to hope. If there was a way to speak to the Earth Mother. If they could send her a gift . . .

'Yes!' Salla's eyes grew round. 'Then She would see . . . She would know . . .'

'She would help us.' Sanna-Leena pressed her face against her baby's cheek. 'The Earth Mother can save us.'

The clan started talking all at once, excited, hopeful.

'I think an Offering is a good idea,' said Helvi quietly. 'I have received many blessings from the Mother. Aurochs Hearth will pledge a gift for the Offering.'

'So will Elk Hearth,' said Jarkko.

'And Reindeer Hearth,' Salla said quickly.

The clan's voices rose again as each Hearth pledged a gift. Tarin reached for the owl feather that still clung desperately to his boot and blew it gently before tucking it into his tunic.

'But how will we give Her the gift?' Saara shook Old Father's arm. 'In the stories you tell, She lives so far away.'

Valo held his hands up for silence once again. 'It will be a long and perilous journey,' he said. Tarin's attention returned to the Spirit Keeper, and his scalp prickled. 'Across the frozen *tundar*, across many rivers, through forests and over mountains – the one chosen to carry the Offering must find the Great Mother's Mountain, Her sacred place.'

'But that is so far,' said Raisa. Her face was pale and she placed her hand on her son's shoulder, drawing him close. 'Whoever is chosen to carry the Offering may never come back.'

'And . . . is that the only way?' Aila asked, her voice soft in the shadows.

'It is the only way,' Valo said. 'The Spirits have said if we do not take this Offering to the Earth Mother, Mammoth Clan is doomed.'

In the stunned silence that followed, the only sound was the moan of the wind through the bones. The cry of the Spirits, the angry, hungry Spirits who covered the earth in ice and brought misfortune to the living.

Tarin's mouth turned dry. The only way . . . the only way to save his clan . . . his family. He tried to speak, but no sound came out.

'But . . . who will take the Offering?' Helvi looked around. 'Each morning, I break the ice on the river to gather water. The days are growing short.'

'We cannot spare one person,' growled Matti. 'If we are to survive the Long Dark, we must hunt every day.'

His voice lowered even further. 'And if any member of the clan thinks to avoid work, then they should not expect a share of the food.'

'And how can you expect the children to hunt.' Aila glared at him. She hugged Saara to her chest.

'I'm not talking about the youngest,' Matti said. Tarin lifted his chin as he felt the man's gaze rest on him.

'I will take the Offering,' said Eero. He stood proudly before the camp and thumped his heavy walking stick into the ground. 'I have made many journeys in my lifetime. I have seen mountains that touch the sky, and glaciers so wide you cannot cross them. I will take one more journey before the Spirits call me.'

'Father, you cannot,' said Jarmo.

'And why not?' The old man glared at his son.

'Because . . .' Jarmo paused and scratched his long beard, unsure what to say.

Silence fell over the camp. Tarin looked around the ring of faces, no longer angry, but filled now with fear. Like the brittle cold of the frozen *tundar*, Tarin could see the fear seeping into their hearts and their bones.

This is all because of me, Tarin thought, and the fear crept into his heart as well. His gaze rested on Saara and Tuuli, and he felt as though his heart would break.

Someone must take the Offering. Tarin's palms felt

sweaty and he rubbed them down the sides of his leggings. His scalp prickled and he felt his mind drifting. It was the feeling he got when he was about to have one of his dreams.

But I'm not sleeping, Tarin thought. This shouldn't be happening. Normally his dreams only came to him when he was alone and snuggled in his furs to sleep, or when Old Mother gave him the strong medicine for his pain. Then he would feel himself lifting up out of his body and floating free, or flying across the frozen landscape on the wings of Spirit of Owl. But not here! Not now!

Tarin forced his eyes open and the strange feeling left him, but not before, for a fleeting moment, he was once again back in the canyon, feeling the touch of the old She-mammoth.

I could take the Offering. The thought came to him suddenly. *I am the one who ruined the hunt. If the camp starves this winter, it is because of me.*

But . . . I cannot. I cannot!

His fears threatened to tear him to pieces with claws as sharp as a cave bear's. From across the fire, Tarin felt Valo's cold, hard stare. He knows about my dreams. He knows how weak I am. And he despises me for it.

Tarin blinked and looked away, unable to return the Spirit Keeper's gaze. A small movement drew his attention to his mother, a pale flutter as her hand touched her throat.

But I am the son of Kalle and Aila, leaders of Mammoth Clan. And I am protected by Spirit of Owl.

The thought gave him strength. Perhaps Jarkko was right. He was a man – if he could just believe in himself.

Tarin cleared his throat and stepped forward. He tried to stand tall and unafraid, when inside, his stomach had shrivelled to a hard, cold lump. But he knew he had to do this – for his family, and for his clan.

'I . . .'

All faces turned to look at him. He knew what they saw. A weak, undersized, scared boy, standing apart and alone.

'I will take the Offering.' His voice cracked. 'I will take the Offering to Great Mother's Mountain. At least . . .' His voice dropped to a whisper. 'At least, I will try.'

'No!' The word burst from Aila's lips. 'No, Tarin must not go.'

'My mother is right.' Taavo shouted to be heard as everyone started to talk at once. 'Why should Tarin have that honour? I am the Firstborn son of the leader of Mammoth Clan. I should be the one to go!'

'The boy will fail . . . again,' said Maija.

'He is weak.'

'But someone must take the Offering.'

The sea of squabbling voices rose around Tarin. His chest felt tight, like it did sometimes when the cold, dry wind blew down from the great ice river in the north. When that happened, Old Mother would brew him a special tea. But there was no comfort for him now. He had to stand in front of his clan and listen to their cruel words.

'Why do you hesitate, Kalle?' Maija asked, her voice as smooth as the sticky sap that flowed from the pine trees, catching unsuspecting insects in its wake. 'Do you doubt the boy can do it? Send your other son, then. Send Taavo.' Her smile widened as still Kalle hesitated.

'Yes, I will go,' said Taavo.

'No!' Tarin spoke firmly, but he was pushed aside as everyone started shouting at once.

'Hear me!' Tarin tried again. Someone's elbow caught him in the chest and he grunted in pain. His hands curled into fists. Why wouldn't they stop and listen to him? And Old Father – he clenched his teeth – why wasn't Old Father doing something, before someone was hurt?

Tarin glared at the old man, sitting back in the shadows, laughing, as the clan's fears built around them. Matti pushed Jarmo in the chest, and the men raised their fists.

Tarin lunged forward and grabbed a handful of Valo's powdered wormwood. He tossed it into the flames and the fire roared towards the roof. The clan screamed and stepped back from the fire.

'No!' Tarin shouted again.

All faces turned towards him. Never before had they heard him shout, and now their shock and surprise showed clearly in the sudden silence.

'Listen to me!' Tarin's voice cut the silence like a spear and he spoke quickly, before he could change his mind, before his fear smothered his anger. 'I will take the Offering. I ruined the mammoth hunt. I have brought shame to my family, and that will never leave me, but . . .' He took a deep breath and as he did, he felt the presence of Owl, clever and wise, watching over him, and he felt the comforting touch of the old She-mammoth, mighty and strong. He no longer felt weak and uncertain. He no longer hung his head in shame.

'I can do this. You think I'll fail, but I won't. I will take the Offering. I will find the Mountain.' He was breathing faster now. 'I am *Haamu* anyway.' He looked at Taavo and Miika, and anger surged through him, hot and wild as a flame. 'And I will return here, to show you all that I made the Offering, and the Earth Mother heard our plea and has forgiven us.'

A strong hand gripped his shoulder.

'Your words are brave, little rabbit,' said Jarkko. 'You have the heart of a hunter, if not the strength.'

'But if he hasn't the strength of a hunter, how can he travel so far?' Taavo muttered. 'It should be me.'

'There is one thing everyone is forgetting.' Jarkko held up his hand before anyone else could speak. 'Tarin was chosen by the Great Mammoth herself.'

'That's right,' said Jarmo. 'I saw Spirit of Mammoth spare him. He should have been crushed.'

'But that wasn't a spirit,' Miika said. 'That was an old mammoth, who was probably blind –'

'Just because someone is old and blind doesn't mean they are mistaken,' said Ilmi, poking Miika in the back with the long deer bone she used as a walking stick. 'If Mammoth has chosen the boy, then let him be the one to take the Offering.'

Voices rose in argument again.

'Enough!' Kalle's giant voice once more demanded silence. He glared at the circle of faces. 'Enough,' he said again, quieter this time. His face looked grey in the fire-light. 'This meeting is finished.' Kalle reached out for the mammoth-bone staff. Three times, he pounded it into the ground. Tarin felt the resounding thud beneath his feet.

'It is decided,' said Old Father, stepping out of the shadows.

The words echoed through Tarin's head, weaving a dance with the hollow sound of bone on bone. The huge mammoth skull drums glowed white in the firelight, shadows flickering, empty eyes staring into the past.

'It is decided,' sang Old Father, drumming the beat with his staff. Sweat ran down his face and he rolled his eyes until all that showed was cloudy white. 'In two days time, at First Light, Tarin of Mammoth Hearth, Son of Kalle, Protected by Spirit of Owl and Chosen by Spirit of Mammoth, shall take the Offering to the Great Mother.'

His eyes returned to normal and he looked at Tarin. 'May the Spirits guide and protect you on your way.'

The Offering

The pendant was made of finely carved bone and strung on a long, leather thong.

'It was my father's.' Aila's voice was soft and low as her hands stroked the smooth bone, tracing the shape of the carving etched deep into the surface. 'See? It has his mark on it.' She placed it gently into Tarin's hand, and he touched the two curved lines meeting in a downwards point – the totem sign of Owl. 'He was a great Spirit Keeper,' Aila said. 'You remind me of him, Tarin. So much.'

'He was lame?' Tarin asked, rolling his eyes. They had had this conversation before.

Aila looked at her son sadly. 'He was kind, and gentle, and brave. Just like you. He cared deeply for his people. You would be a good Spirit Keeper, Tarin. Better than Valo. He knows that, and that's why he fears you.'

Tarin made a surprised sound. 'Valo fears me? How does

he fear anything when he faces the bad Spirits every day? How could he fear me?' Tarin shook his head. He didn't understand what his mother meant. He closed his hand around the pendant. 'I'm not brave enough to be a Spirit Keeper,' he said finally.

Aila sighed. 'There are different kinds of bravery.' She rested her hand on one of the large mammoth bones that formed the wall of the lodge and stroked it. 'Twelve summers ago, you were born here, Tarin. Here in this lodge. Barely a year after Taavo.'

Tarin nodded. He had heard the story before. How his life had started too soon within his mother.

'They said I couldn't care for two babies. Old Mother gave me the secret herbs to stop your life, but still you lived. Then when you were born they said you were weak and would never survive.' Aila paused and closed her eyes, breathing deeply. 'I fought them when they took you, Tarin. I fought them so hard. I screamed and kicked and tore at their flesh with my bare hands.' She opened her eyes and stared at her hands, now curled into clawed talons. 'Valo picked me up and carried me away. I had to leave you there, on the rocks at the top of the canyon. You were supposed to die. But still, you lived!' She gripped Tarin's shoulders and shook him. 'You know this.'

Tarin nodded, but the words wouldn't come. He had

heard his tale so many times.

Asa had stayed, to bear witness to his fate. She saw the wolverine come sniffing around the tiny, twisted body, scenting blood and weakness. She saw its strong jaws reach out to clamp around his throat, to silence his cry, and she called to the Spirits to take the baby quickly. Then Owl came plummeting down from the sky, claws outstretched to strike Wolverine across the face.

It was the will of the Spirits, Asa said, and she had gathered him up and rushed back to the clan. Valo had decreed her *Haamu* for a full moon cycle.

'You should have died, Tarin. Three times over. But still you lived. Owl is your totem, your protector, brave and strong, silent and wise. Just like you.'

Tarin shook his head. 'I'm not wise. I'm not brave or strong.' His voice wavered and he dropped his head.

'Sometimes,' Aila said, 'strength can be found in the smallest creatures. A wolverine can bring down a musk ox. A fox can take a baby. A man can fell a mammoth. And you, Tarin, my son ...' She paused and brushed his hair from his face. Tarin shook his head until it once more covered his eyes. Aila smiled. 'You, my son, are strong in ways we have yet to see.' She tilted Tarin's face up to hers, to look deep into his eyes. Tarin saw the sparkle of unshed tears. 'My father also went on a long journey when he was a young man. He was gone for many years . . .' Her voice wavered and faded away. Her hands dropped and she turned away.

Sadness stuck in Tarin's throat like a lump of ice. He was about to undertake a great journey, and perhaps he would never again see his mother, or his father, or any of his family. Perhaps he would never return to Mammoth Clan. The thought made his chest hurt and his eyes sting.

Tarin reached his hand towards his mother, sitting so still.

'Return to me, Tarin. Let me look on your face one more time,' she pleaded softly.

Tarin put the leather thong about his neck and felt the weight of the Owl pendant against his chest. It was warm to touch, warmed by his mother's hand.

'I will see you again, Mother.' Tarin felt the weight of the promise in his words and his hand trembled as he reached to grasp her shoulder, in the way of their clan.

A sob escaped Aila. She pulled Tarin to her and hugged him to her chest. Tarin knew that as a man he should stand tall and brave. Not cry. Not show weakness. But he felt his own arms returning her embrace, and he buried his head in her hair, breathing in her scent. Then, with a shuddering sigh, Aila pushed him gently away, and Tarin's arms felt suddenly empty and bereft.

'I will see you again, Tarin,' she whispered.

'I will see you again, Mother,' Tarin replied, and he turned and left the earth-lodge.

The Offering was wrapped in a thick snow leopard fur given by Mammoth Hearth.

Soft leathers from Reindeer Hearth.

A grass-wrapped parcel of food from Aurochs Hearth.

Two carved ivory beads from Fox Hearth.

A cave bear tooth from Bear Hearth.

A flint blade from Elk Hearth.

Herbs from Old Mother.

From Ilmi, who knew her time on this earth was short, a small piece of amber, a tiny ant trapped inside. Her special gift to the Earth Mother, to ask protection for the family she would leave behind.

And in his hand, Tarin carried a tall, straight spear, carved by his father and tipped with the special bone spear point that Taavo had made Tarin for his first hunt.

It was the hour before dawn when Tarin climbed to the granite rocks that jutted out over the river. Taavo sat with his back against a rock, looking out at the windswept steppes beyond. Below them, the five rounded earth-lodges huddled forlornly on a wide terrace above the river.

Tarin stood and watched the first rays of light turn the

grasslands from grey to palest pink. He didn't know what to say to his brother, who sat so silently.

'Taavo ...' Tarin waited until his brother looked at him. Taavo's eyes were red, but the wind was blowing the loess dust from the edge of the glacier, and Tarin knew his eyes were raw as well.

'Everything is different now, Tarin.' Taavo's voice cracked and he turned once more to look out at the horizon. 'We were supposed to hunt together, you and I ...' He picked up a stone and threw it angrily. Both boys watched it arc in the air before falling towards the rushing river.

Soon, the water would slow to a trickle, then stop altogether, as the Ice Mother tightened her grip on the land. Tarin brushed tangled hair out of his eyes and looked down at the earth-lodges. In the grey light of dawn, figures appeared, some to carry water, some to gather bone and dung to fuel the fires. Some started to climb the hill towards them. They moved easily, striding over the rocky ground in a way Tarin never could. He recognised Miika, and his heart sank. Today, he didn't need to see his sneering face, or hear the contempt in his voice. He didn't need Miika to remind him he was tall and strong and Tarin was ... not.

Three smaller figures followed him – Pia, Erik and Niko. All younger than Tarin, yet they would be hunters soon, leaving him to dig his plants and gather grains with his sisters. Taavo watched them, too, the angry scowl on his face deepening. He rose to his feet and dusted off his leggings.

'It should be my journey.' His voice was a growl. 'I am the son of Kalle. And one day, it will be my turn to be leader. I should be the one to take the Offering, not you.' He glared at Tarin. The anger in his eyes made him a stranger to his brother.

'I am Kalle's son as well,' Tarin said, but the wind swept his voice away. He held his hand out to his brother, longing to be children again, tumbling through the grass in search of birds to scare and sweet berries to eat. But Taavo pushed it away.

'You've changed everything, Tarin. It should be me saving the clan. Instead, you are going and I am staying here to dig marmots and stoats out of holes in the ground, and with luck, I might be able to spear a *baybaka* through its ugly head and claim my right to be a hunter of Mammoth Clan.' Taavo's voice rose angrily. He waved his hands in the air. 'Can you imagine the songs that will be sung for me? The great hunter who single-handedly brought down the mighty lemming or the savage hamster?'

Tarin shook his head, unsure what to say.

'Taavo!' Miika called as he approached. He shouldered Tarin aside without a glance, and placed a hand around

Taavo's shoulder. 'I am planning a hunt. They say reindeer are still in the valley past the bend in the river. Do you come?'

'I . . . I must farewell my brother,' said Taavo.

'Why waste your time?' Miika's gaze flicked over Tarin's face.

Taavo scowled and rubbed his nose. 'I must. My father expects me to.'

'Of course we must see Tarin off.' Pia pushed her brother playfully and laughed when Miika frowned. Tarin was glad Pia hadn't forgotten their old friendship, and he opened his mouth to thank her, when she continued. 'We can all laugh when he starts crying.' She turned her pale blue eyes on him and they were like shards of ice from the great glacier. 'You are scared, aren't you, Tarin? I've heard you cry out sometimes, during the night. You cry like one of the babies. Like Maikki, or Niko here.' She ruffled the hair of the younger boy standing next to her. Niko frowned and tried to stand taller. Erik and Miika laughed.

Tarin clenched his teeth and felt his hands curl into fists. How could he tell her he cried out when the dreams came to him – the dreams of darkness and falling and cold earth pressing down, squeezing the breath from his body? How could he tell her he cried out when Old Mother pulled his leg to straighten it and make it strong? How, even with the special herbs to dull the pain and take his spirit from his body, he could still feel his bones grate against each other and his muscles tear and twist.

'I'm not a baby,' cried Niko. 'I can count ten summers now, and Miika is going to teach me how to hunt. I can already use a sling better than you.'

'Ha!' said Pia with a snort. 'A sling is a baby's weapon. To be a hunter, you have to use a spear.' She hefted her spear in her hand. 'But you can't even use a sling, can you, Tarin? How do you think you are going to survive by yourself?'

'He won't,' Miika snarled. 'He will die, and our Offering will be lost. Because of him, our clan will perish ...'

Without warning, he pushed Tarin backwards.

Rocks shifted beneath Tarin's feet and he sat down abruptly, jarring every bone in his body.

'That's enough,' said Taavo. He tried to hold Miika back, but the older boy was stronger and heavier, and for a moment it looked as though he would push Taavo to the ground as well. 'You have no right to criticise my brother.'

'This is my right.' Miika spat the words. His eyes blazed and he ripped his tunic down over his left shoulder, exposing his hunter's tattoo – three parallel lines, as though a great bear had ripped his flesh. 'This is my right. I am a hunter of Mammoth Clan. Miika of Aurochs Hearth, protected by Bear.' He turned his eyes on Tarin and Tarin felt the hate blazing out of them. 'That ... that ... weakling ... will never be a man. He will never be a hunter of Mammoth Clan. And if you, or your father, think otherwise, then perhaps it is time Mammoth Clan had a new leader.'

'What do you mean?' Taavo pushed his chin out and glared at Miika. The older boy looked him up and down.

'I thought you were different, Taavo. I thought you had what it takes to be a man. But I was mistaken.' Miika shook his head and turned away. He flicked his hand and Pia, Erik and Niko followed him.

'What do you mean by that!' Taavo screamed after him, his face red and his fists clenched.

'Taavo . . .' Tarin's voice was hoarse. 'Let him go.' He grabbed his brother's shoulder, but Taavo shook him off.

'This is all your fault!' he shouted into Tarin's face. Tarin felt a warm spray of spittle as Taavo tried desperately to control his rage. 'And Miika is right. You are going to fail. We will all die here, this Winter, and it's all because of you.'

His words were like a physical blow and Tarin stepped back.

'Taavo, you are my brother. We can't part like this . . .'

'Just go, Tarin. Go on your great journey, and . . . and . . .' He stopped speaking and dropped his head, his shoulders shaking as he drew in large gulps of air.

Tarin stared helplessly at him. 'I . . . I will see you again.' He reached out again to grip Taavo's shoulder.

'No!' Taavo stepped back, his hand raised. His mouth twisted and he dashed a hand across his eyes. 'No, Tarin. Go! I do not wish to see you again.' And then he turned and ran, back towards the granite rocks that sat silent and brooding above the camp.

Tarin made his way carefully down to the river. A stepping rock wobbled under his foot as he crossed the shallow water to the small, rocky beach on the other side. Most of Mammoth Clan had assembled there to farewell him, but Tarin was sure some had come to see him falter and slip on the rocks. He wondered how many of them had seen and heard what his brother had said.

'Good journey,' said Jarkko. He stepped forward and pressed a small packet into his hands. 'Some travelling food for you – dried reindeer mixed with juniper berries and fat. It is what we eat when we go hunting.'

Tarin looked up at the tall man. His sister, Tuuli, stood next to him, her eyes red. Words swelled in his throat, but he couldn't speak. He pressed his lips together, afraid that if he opened them, sounds of fear would escape.

The wind blew ice cold and he shivered. Snow was in the air, and soon a blanket of white would cover the hills and plains. Already the mammoth and the woolly rhinoceros were gone, hurrying towards their winter grounds, away from the deep snows.

Snow birds were turning from nut brown to white. Hares, jerboas and marmots scurried around frantically, searching for the last few elusive nuts to store before they, too, fled to their hidden burrows to wait out *Kaamos*. Tarin pulled his fur *beaska*, his coat, tightly around his body.

'I will walk with you a way,' Kalle said gruffly. He picked up Tarin's pack and swung it onto his own broad back. Tarin looked at his father in surprise, but Kalle was already striding ahead. Tarin only had time to raise his hand once in farewell before hurrying after him.

'You will make for Bison Clan, by the fork of the big river. We are kin, and they will feed you and set you on your way. Mind though, you will need to cross the river at Two Rock Peak.'

'Yes, Father.' Tarin's chest felt tight and his breath was sharp. His father's long legs covered the ground rapidly, and he hurried after him.

'Then you will make for Musk Ox Clan. They will be camped at their Winter grounds near the edge of the *tundar*. Kai is wintering with them. You remember Hanno's son? He is thinking of apprenticing to the Musk Ox Spirit Keeper. It would be a fine thing for him. Hanno and Salla are very lucky. He is a son to be proud of.'

A son to be proud of . . .

Kalle's words cut wounds into Tarin's heart, but he didn't

speak. He needed all his breath to keep pace with his father as the ground rose and became steeper. He used the spear to balance himself over the rocky trail.

Kalle waited impatiently at the top of the incline. He eyed his son seriously and stroked his long red beard. Tarin followed the movement of his hand as he caught his breath. Today, Kalle's beard was twisted into three parts, a leather thong wound around each.

'The days are already short.' Kalle cleared his throat and looked out at the plains, a deep furrow between his bushy eyebrows. 'If you have not reached the Mountain in two Moons, you must Winter with Musk Ox Clan. The snow will be too thick on the ground, even with snow-shoes.'

Tarin nodded, but his voice stuck in his throat. He wished he had some of Old Mother's special tea to make his breathing easier.

'They will look after you.' Kalle rubbed his nose and tugged his beard. 'I am inclined to journey part way with you,' he murmured, watching his son carefully.

Tarin shrugged his shoulders and looked out over the rolling hills. Somewhere in the hazy distance was the big river, and past that were the mountains. He realised his father was waiting for an answer, and considered his words. Was this a test? he wondered.

If Jarkko or Matti were here, they would laugh and slap

Kalle on the back and tell him such an old man as he would slow them down. Kalle would laugh, too, and slap them back. But if he slaps me on the back, Tarin mused, I will fly through the air like a plover chick learning to fly. He scratched his nose and shuffled his feet. Above him, a bird – a hawk maybe, or an eagle owl – circled high. Tarin felt like it was watching him.

'Father,' he said, then he hesitated.

There was so much he wanted to say, but standing there on the edge of Mammoth Clan territory, the vast steppes before him, his words seemed too small for what was in his heart. He wished, so much, to just turn and run back to camp. His feet shuffled, and almost turned homewards.

But that will not help my clan, he thought. The way ahead was long and uncertain, but he felt that Spirit of Owl was very close to him. He raised his face to the wind and it lifted his hair into a wild tangle. He drew in a deep breath and the air was chill. This was his journey – and his alone. He would not let his fears overwhelm him, and he would not be responsible for Mammoth Clan losing another strong hunter.

He stood tall, wobbling only a little on his weak leg. 'Father, I will see you again.' Tarin looked at him, but didn't dare to reach for his shoulder.

Kalle rubbed his beard and the back of his neck, then

nodded, as though a decision had been reached. 'Valo told me the journey was yours. I think he is right.'

'Old Father would say he is always right,' Tarin said.

He was surprised when Kalle laughed. Tarin laughed too in sheer joy. The bleakness that had smothered him since the mammoth hunt lifted from his heart. His journey was before him. The open grasslands of the plains, the undulating fields of golden, brittle hay and, in the far distance, a line of bent and twisted trees – pine, alder and birch. In the forests, these trees would grow to be giants. On the steppes, where the constant winds from the glacier stunted their growth, they huddled along riverbanks and ravines.

'I will see you again, little rab . . . Tarin. I will see you again, Tarin – my son.' Kalle reached forward, as though to hug Tarin to his chest, but then he stopped. With his right hand, he gripped his son's shoulder instead. Tarin felt his bones crunch beneath his father's grip.

Kalle sniffed and stepped back. 'Good journey.'

Tarin nodded, unable to speak. He knew if he did the tears would run from his eyes, and he would be less of a man. Instead, he shouldered his pack, grasped his spear, and started down the hill towards the open steppes.

His journey would be long, and hard. He knew that. But he would continue across the plains until he reached the big river. At night, he would set up his aurochs hide tent and sleep wrapped in his sleeping furs of softest fox pelts. In the small streams crossing his path he would replenish his water flask, and he had enough food to last until he reached Bison Clan.

Tarin paused before his trail turned and looked back the way he had come. His father still stood on the top of the hill, his hand raised in farewell. His other hand was lifted to his eyes, but whether to shield his gaze from the rising sun, or to wipe the dust from his eyes, Tarin couldn't tell. He raised his own hand and suddenly felt very alone.

A shift in the wind urged him onwards. Tarin turned, letting his feet carry him forward across the plains. Away from his father. Away from his clan. And away from his home.

Boar Clan

Kaija ran, her feet sinking deep into drifts of fallen pine needles. Branches scratched her face and clawed her hair, but she dared not stop. The sounds of pursuit, although fainter, were still behind her. She rubbed the ache in her side and kept running.

'Kaija! Wait!'

'Luuka, come on!' Kaija slowed as her brother struggled to match her pace. 'They are right behind us.'

'Wait!'

She turned impatiently towards him and hissed in frustration. The two rabbit carcasses slung around his neck were caught in the low branches of a blackthorn thicket.

'Leave them!'

Luuka shook his head, his mouth a firm, thin line. 'No. We have to eat.'

'And if they catch us, they'll string us up like those

rabbits.' Kaija bent over to relieve the pain in her side and drew in large gulps of air. Her mouth twisted. 'Our lives are not worth those pathetic scraps of meat. I've seen more flesh on . . . on a mosquito.'

Luuka shrugged and looked at the rabbits. His fingers stroked the soft fur. 'We need to eat,' he repeated. 'And how can Boar Clan say we stole their meat? They don't own the forest. No one owns the forest!'

'I know that. But things are different here.' Kaija ran her hand through her hair and rubbed her face, smearing it with dirt and sweat. 'We're a long way from home.'

Luuka nodded, his shoulders slumped. Kaija's heart sank at the angry, closed look in his eyes – a look that hadn't been there before they had to flee, a look that hadn't been there until Retu died.

'We don't have a home anymore, Kaija. Remember?'

Kaija shook her head and closed her eyes. Nightmare images rose before her, and she was back in the cave.

Angry voices in the night . . . fear, like a mist, seeping into every darkened crevice . . . the smell of sickness and burning willowbark . . .

Then their flight from River Clan, and the fear-filled days that had followed. Always hungry. Always watchful. Deeper and deeper into the forest they had run, leaving behind all that was familiar. They'd foraged for nuts and grubbed for mushrooms and moss. At night they'd huddled together, barely sleeping, while wolves and other night creatures scented weakness and lurked in the shadows, waiting. They had driven them off with flames and stones, but the predators scented their weakness and bided their time.

Finally, Luuka's traps had snared two pitiful rabbits, all bone and fur.

Kaija rubbed her face in anger. That was when the Boar Clan hunting party had appeared out of nowhere, calling them thieves and pushing Luuka to the ground. They were big, strong men and women, armed with short spears. They should have dropped the rabbits. Kaija realised that now. They should have begged for help. Instead, hunger and anger and stubbornness had made them run.

A cry and a shout to their left shattered her thoughts. They had been seen.

'Run!' Kaija pushed her brother before her.

Fear surged through her, lending speed to her feet. She barely registered the uneven ground, the exposed roots and rocks that threatened to trip her. She was only aware of the fear inside her and her brother in front of her, two dead rabbits bouncing around his neck.

A sound rushed past Kaija's ear and she stumbled, confused. Were there birds here in the forest that swooped and hunted their prey? She glanced upward but saw only the deep green pine trees towering overhead, their branches dusted in light snow. She heard another shout, this time closer. Voices closed in from both sides.

A loose rock beneath her feet saved her life. Kaija felt the rocks move ... and then she was falling down a small embankment. Another of the bird sounds rushed past her and a short spear thudded into the tree above her. An icy shiver ran down her spine. How can a man throw a spear with such force that it lodges itself in a tree? She found herself unable to drag her eyes from the sight of the spear firmly stuck in the wood even though danger was closing in. She heard it in the shouting voices and the sounds of pounding feet.

She pushed herself up and felt a twinge in her ankle. Voices drifted down the embankment. Kaija looked around frantically. She saw a fallen tree, overgrown with brambles, and dived towards it. Thorny briars scratched her hands and face, but she pushed herself further into them and burrowed into the thick layer of rotting leaf matter and old wood. It crumbled easily at her touch, covering her in a coat of mulch. Deeper and deeper she burrowed, close to panic. The sound of the pursuers scrambling down the embankment was frighteningly close. She clenched her muscles to stop herself from trembling and forced herself to lie still.

'The little brat is hiding somewhere,' a rough voice said.

Kaija heard the sounds of undergrowth being searched and heavy tramping. Snatches of laughter came to her, but she couldn't hear what they were saying. The sound of her pounding heart echoed so loudly in her head, she thought the whole forest would hear it. She closed her eyes and felt fresh sweat break out on her body. It stung her scratches and made her itch. Her lungs screamed for air, but the musty smell of the leaf litter and loamy earth irritated her nose and throat. Kaija held her breath and sent a silent plea to her totem protector.

Spirit of Horse, hide me, please. Keep me safe.

A man stopped by her log. He reeked of sweat and rancid meat. Kaija felt her stomach churn.

'Thieves,' he muttered. 'Dirty thieves.' And he spat on the ground.

A small sound escaped from Kaija's lips, but the man didn't notice.

We are not thieves, she repeated to herself, over and over. She forced herself to lie still. *We are not thieves, and we have just as much right to hunt in the forest as you do.*

A call came from deeper in the forest, and the hunter moved off.

Kaija lay very still, straining her ears to hear. The forest was silent. Carefully, she raised her head and looked around, but there was no one there. Tears streamed down her cheeks, mixing with the mud and stale sweat. Her muscles trembled and she had no strength left to move. A howl rose in her throat, like a physical pain. It tore her heart apart, and she curled into a ball and lay sobbing on the forest floor, sobbing for all she had lost.

Hours later, weary and frightened, Kaija crawled from her hiding place and pushed herself to her feet. She dusted the dirt from her clothes. Her empty stomach clenched and she swayed, suddenly light-headed. She scrambled back up the embankment on her hands and knees, forcing her weary limbs to climb. She had to find Luuka.

The last time she saw him, before she fell, he was running ahead of her, veering to the right. She studied the scene around her, taking note of the broken branches and disturbed earth. She was good at tracking – one of the best in her clan – but fear clouded her mind and made her hands shake. She rubbed her aching head and wished she could think clearly. 'Luuka, where are you?' she whispered. Her voice was swallowed by the silent forest.

She found a trail and followed it. Someone had definitely passed this way. Her hand brushed the dark green pine leaves. Someone had run this way, dislodging the covering of snow from the branches and leaving their footprints in the soft earth. She knelt to examine a cluster of low-growing club-moss, crushed by a heavy tread. A tuft of grey fur fluttered from the jutting branch of a spindle tree. Rabbit fur. At shoulder height. A curtain of beard-moss lay torn from a graceful spruce tree, as though someone had blundered into it as they ran with unseeing eyes.

A sliver of dread pierced Kaija's heart. She closed her eyes and tried to quell the rising panic.

'Spirit of Horse, protect your child,' she murmured under her breath. 'Please help him.'

She always felt Spirit of Horse was a better totem for herself than for Luuka. She yearned to run wild and free, while he was happiest near the water, diving off rocks as sure-footed as an otter. But they had shared a womb, so their totem was the same. 'Help him run like the wind.'

Kaija followed the signs to a small clearing. She paused and looked around, her breath steaming the air, her blood pounding through her body. A light dusting of snow covered the ground, now trampled and sullied with the heavy tread of many men. Their larger footprints almost completely obliterated the smaller, lighter tread of their quarry. There had been a fight here, Kaija realised, the icy hand about her heart squeezing tighter. She knelt by a depression in the ground, made by a falling body. Two dark red drops of blood stained a nearby rock. Kaija felt faint.

'Luuka . . .' His name was a cry of anguish on her dry lips. Her gaze followed the furrows in the snow where something, or someone, was dragged. Kaija sat on the ground and dropped her head onto her knees. She felt very alone.

Something brushed against her face and she looked up to find snowflakes falling gently. They settled on her hair and caught in her eyelashes. She brushed them away impatiently. Snow would cover the tracks, she realised. And then how would she follow Luuka?

The thought made her stop and think. Was that what she was going to do? Follow the Boar Clan tracks back to their camp? And then what? Could she possibly rescue Luuka alone?

She shivered and wrapped her arms tightly around her knees. But what was the alternative? To desert her brother? To carry on without him? It was unthinkable.

But I don't even know if he's still alive!

Kaija cried aloud at the idea of losing her twin. It couldn't happen – not after all they had been through. She crouched in the clearing and rocked back and forth, a low wailing sound escaping from her lips.

He can't be dead. Please don't let him be dead.

She saw him again in her mind, clutching his rabbits, determination etched into his face.

'We need to eat, Kaija.'

She closed her eyes and felt hot tears flow down her cheeks. She had been the one who'd convinced Luuka this was a good place to hunt. He had set the snares only because starvation stared them in the face and they were hopelessly lost. She had no idea where Beaver Clan was. She no longer even knew where the river was.

She realised she was staring at a patch of disturbed snow near where Luuka had fallen. She blinked her eyes and frowned, a wave of nausea hitting her as she realised she was staring at the rabbit carcasses, lying trampled and discarded on the ground.

She picked up the rabbits and held them to her chest, now little more than pathetic scraps of bloodied fur.

'Luuka!' she cried, no longer worried that her voice would be heard. But there was only silence under the trees. The snow kept falling, blanketing her in white. 'Luuka!' she cried again, but there was no one left to hear her.

She was alone in the forest, with two bloodied corpses clutched in her hand.

It was nearly dark when Kaija forced herself to move. She didn't know how long she had sat there, as the snow fell around her in thickening drifts. How easy it would be, she thought, to just stay here. She could lie down in one of the drifts and simply go to sleep.

But who would save Luuka?

The thought was like a small flame inside, urging her to stand and brush the snow from her furs. It urged her to move her stiff, unwilling limbs and look for shelter. Without shelter, she wouldn't survive the night.

Her feet led her back into the forest, away from the small clearing. The movement warmed her blood, but already her fingers and toes were numb. Salty tears stung her scratched face. She was thirsty, but she knew she only had a small amount of water left in her water flask. Instead, she scooped a handful of snow and let it melt in her mouth.

Only if you must . . .

Kaija gasped as her mother's voice spoke to her.

Only if you must . . . and beware . . . the snow will take the fire from your blood and make it cold. Sister Snow is jealous of our life-fire . . .

'Mother?' Kaija cried aloud. She turned, searching the shadows, but there was nothing there. She forced her cold, aching feet to move. Time lost all meaning and the sky darkened.

'Shelter . . . I have to find . . .' She paused and squinted into the shadows. A darker shadow loomed before her. Eager, she stumbled forward, falling on hands and knees in her haste. She reached the rocky outcrop and cried aloud in relief. It wasn't a cave, but sometime in the past a landslide had sent large granite boulders crashing down the mountainside. A cavity had formed where they had come to rest, big enough to provide shelter from the snow and icy wind.

Kaija huddled thankfully against the rocks. No snow could fall here, and she was happy to burrow her frozen feet into the soft ground cover of fallen leaves. She cleared a small circle of debris and ringed it in stones. From a pouch inside her furs, she drew her fire-sticks and the leaf litter provided perfect tinder. Kaija placed one pointed fire-stick into a depression in the other and started to twirl.

It was difficult by herself – usually she and Luuka would take turns twirling the fire-stick downwards, alternating in rhythm so the stick was always spinning. By the time a wisp of smoke rose from the tinder beneath, Kaija felt warm. She leaned close and blew gently on the smouldering ember, carefully feeding the infant flame. To her relief, the flame grew. A tree, shattered by the falling boulders, provided plenty of fuel for her fire.

Kaija sipped carefully from her water flask and considered her situation.

She didn't think Luuka was dead – not yet. Boar Clan wouldn't bother carrying a dead body back to their camp. That meant he must be a prisoner. The snow would destroy their tracks, but she knew what direction they were heading. Tomorrow, she would follow.

For how long? The question flashed through her mind unbidden.

'For as long as it takes.' She said the words fiercely, and felt better to hear them spoken aloud.

But still, that inner voice needled her.

You're not prepared for a long journey. You were supposed to be at Beaver camp by now, asking for help.

'I have my knife, my sling . . .' Kaija countered, eyeing the darkness as she made her plans. 'I don't have enough water. I don't have a spear. My clothes need drying. I have no idea where I am . . .' Her foot moved and kicked the rabbit carcasses. A small smile twisted her lips. 'I have two fine rabbits, which I will skin in the morning.' She shivered as she felt the wind change direction. 'And I'm alive.' Two days ago, she hadn't expected to be.

Her hand crept to the leather thong around her neck. She clutched the pendant of carved bone.

Her mother's totem was Spirit of Snow Leopard. It was a strong totem, yet even Snow Leopard hadn't protected them. Could Spirit of Horse help her?

Kaija felt her eyes droop. She was so tired. She had been running forever . . .

She stared into the dancing flames, letting images flicker through her mind. She was scratched and bleeding, cold and thirsty. Misery overwhelmed her and tears flowed unchecked down her cheeks. She cried for her mother, and her home – for everything she had lost. And she cried for herself, alone in the forest.

Finally, exhausted, Kaija slept.

The Journey
Begins

The light was almost gone from the sky and the first few stars were appearing overhead when Tarin decided to make camp. He had walked steadily all day, over rolling hills and across the plains, but the mountains never seemed to grow closer. The last hill he had climbed had been steep, the rocks uneven beneath his feet, and now he stood on the ridge top and looked towards the horizon, breathing hard.

'Keep the rising sun before you, and you should reach the big river in two days,' his father had said. Tarin squinted in the fading light, but all he could see were more hills and more waving grass. Below him, a herd of saiga antelope paused to graze. They lifted long noses towards him and sniffed the air, wary of his human scent. Nervously they moved on, the clatter of their hoofs startling a ptarmigan to flight. Tarin watched the bird, its mottled feathers turning from summer brown to winter white, as it flew away.

'Then I turn north,' he whispered to himself, echoing his father's words. He pictured Kalle sitting on a rock before the cooking pit, scratching shapes in the dirt with a long deer bone.

'After Bison Clan, follow the river until you reach the place where it flows into the ground. For one day's journey, the river flows beneath the earth, hidden from sight. It is one of the wonders of the Earth Mother.'

'Why can't I just give the Offering to the river then?' Tarin had asked, but his father shook his head.

'Old Father has asked the Spirits, and he says you have to take the Offering to Great Mother's Mountain, to the cave called the Mother's Heart. It is there you will give the Offering to the Earth Mother, and she will give you a token in return.'

The evening breeze lifted Tarin's sweaty hair off his face and he shivered. The light had dimmed further as he stood lost in thought, and his stomach growled. He decided not to set up his tent. Instead, he would make a fire and sleep rolled in his sleeping furs, gazing at the stars above.

A thrill of excitement warmed his blood. It would be his first night spent alone, away from the earth-lodge, and away from his family.

He stood at the top of the ridge and opened his arms wide, as though to embrace the endless steppes before him. He drew in a large breath of cold air, lifted his face to the sky, and yelled. 'Hei . . . yo!'

His cry sounded louder in the quiet of early evening.

'Hei! Hei! Hei!' he shouted again, listening to the way his voice carried across the plains.

There was no answering cry. He was completely alone.

Tarin drew his breath in sharply. At Mammoth Camp, there was always someone close by, especially in summer when the whole clan would travel to forage and hunt. Then, they would all sleep in the one large tent, and often there were other tents and other clans joining them. Furs and bone would be traded for dried fish and shells. Or simply for good company and stories and songs long into the summer night, when the sun barely left the sky.

But out here on the steppes, on the edge of winter, there were no people snoring or talking quietly to each other. There were no soft baby cries, or the sounds and smells of cooking and sharing a meal. A lump rose in Tarin's throat as he waited in vain for an answer to his call. The smile left his face and his shoulders sagged. In that moment, he understood what exile truly meant.

Then, from far away, came the call of a wolf. The familiar sound cheered Tarin, but it also reminded him of the many predators that lived on the steppes. Wolves, hyenas, wolverines, dholes, and the giant cave lions. A young boy alone would be an easy target. His gaze darted to the darker shadows cast by a small copse of stunted trees, almost expecting to see shining eyes and the gleam of white teeth. But there was nothing there.

Tarin fumbled in his pack for his fire-lighting kit, and quickly made a circle of stones. He dug a small depression in the middle and filled it with tinder – dried fungus and the fuzz of old bulrush stalks. The trees yielded a pile of larger twigs and branches, which Tarin placed next to his fireplace.

Out of a leather pouch, he took his fire-lighting stones. He weighed them in his hands. He had never actually lit a fire from the stones before, although he had seen it done many times. No one had thought it important for Tarin to learn. Mammoth Camp always had fires going, and it was easier to borrow a coal from another fire than to light a new one. But he knew the hunters and traders all carried firestones to light their fires when they were away from home.

Tarin closed his eyes, picturing his mother striking the stones together ... drawing the spark ... and blowing gently until the flame grew strong. For a moment, he was back in the earth-lodge with her, the familiar sights and smells filling his mind. He saw his mother raise her head and smile at him. The lump in his throat throbbed painfully.

Tarin opened his eyes.

He wasn't in his earth-lodge, and his mother wasn't there to soothe his fears. He was alone, in the middle of the plains, and night was falling.

With shaking hands, he struck the stones together.

The first time, nothing happened.

He struck a second time, adjusting the angle, and this time a spark flew. It fell onto the dried fungus, and Tarin quickly bent to blow the spark. A wisp of smoke rose, followed by the glow of a flame.

He felt warmth against his face and smelled the scent of burning bark. A small red tongue flickered in the nest, eagerly devouring the dry tinder. Carefully, he fed the larger pieces of wood, watching as the flame grew bigger.

Tarin's mouth stretched into a wide smile. He could almost imagine the countless predators of the plains retreating in the face of such a bright, burning light.

He held his hands out towards the flame and watched a spiral of grey smoke rise upwards to the stars. He rummaged once more in his pack, and brought out a grass-wrapped packet of dried meat and currants.

Tarin recalled the worried look on his father's face. 'We can't spare you much food,' said Kalle. 'We have little in store. But this will see you to Bison Camp, and they will provide more for you.'

Tarin looked down at the packet in his hands and swallowed hard. He thought of the hunger his clan would feel that winter, and coldness settled again in the pit of his stomach. Once more he heard Valo's voice.

Mammoth Clan is doomed. The Spirits have spoken.

'I won't let that happen,' Tarin said. 'Somehow . . . I will find Great Mother's Mountain and Mother's Heart.'

The wind dropped, and even the crackling fire quietened, as though to hear his words. He took a small bite of the dried reindeer meat and chewed, but he was no longer hungry. The meat was tough and Tarin sipped water from his flask to help him swallow. He nibbled at the currants, then wrapped the rest up and stowed it away in his pack.

'I cannot fail,' Tarin murmured. He wrapped his sleeping furs around himself and thought about his journey. All the way to the mountains – it seemed so far. But surely Old Father wouldn't have let him go if he had no chance of succeeding? Would he?

Tarin wasn't sure. If he failed, then Mammoth Clan would have one less mouth to feed. The thought didn't comfort him. He lay back and stared up at the inky sky studded with bright points of light.

He remembered a story his mother once told him, about

how the stars were the hearth fires of all those who had gone to the next world. There were so many of them. He wondered if any of them had belonged to Mammoth Clan. Maybe Ristak's hearth fire was there somewhere. And all the other members of Mammoth Clan that had died. And then he couldn't help thinking – If I die, out here, away from my home, how will my mother know? Will she look up into the sky and see my fire? How will she know which fire is mine?

Tears welled in Tarin's eyes and he brushed them away. Another wolf howl echoed across the steppes, closer this time.

Tarin shivered and added more wood to his fire. Sparks rose skywards, then settled. His body was exhausted, but his eyes wouldn't close. They stared at the dancing flames, seeing images and pictures there.

The night would be long, he thought, and the days short. In just over two cycles of the moon, the sun would barely rise over the edge of the earth.

'You must be with Musk Ox Clan or Bison Clan by then,' he murmured to himself. 'You won't survive the Winter alone.' A branch cracked and shifted in the fire, but by that time the tension in his body was easing and his eyes were closing. Sleep finally overtook him.

'Where are you?' Tarin was standing in the middle of an endless plain, surrounded by head-high feather grass. 'I can't find you!'

A wolf was running – a wolf with a dark band of fur around one ankle. He knew her fear. It was like a bitter taste in his mouth. A bright light hurt his eyes, and he snarled and snapped at it. Was he the wolf? He growled deep in his throat. He was afraid not only for himself, but for the two small pups cowering in their den. The light came closer. Voices shouted. Hands reached for him.

Tarin woke with a start, bathed in sweat. First light was just breaking.

Morning dawned grey and cold. Fitful clouds scudded across a leaden sky. Kaija rose unrefreshed. Nightmare images had filled her dreams. Fierce faces streaked with red ochre and grey ash. Dead rabbits, flies clustered around their sightless eyes, pus-filled boils covering their bodies. And in the moments before waking, there had been a wolf running ...

Kaija rubbed her eyes and stared in distaste at the rabbit carcasses still waiting to be skinned and cooked. Luuka had risked his life for those rabbits. She swallowed her nausea and forced herself to clean and spit the scrawny animals. There was little meat left on them, and she picked what she could off the bones. At least it was some food in her belly, she told herself, but when she tried to swallow, her stomach heaved and the stringy meat stuck in her throat. With a great effort, she forced a small mouthful down, followed by a sip of water. Then she cracked the bones and sucked the rich marrow.

Kaija sat back on her haunches and held her aching head. How did the sickness start, she wondered? Headache ... aching limbs ... chills ... vomiting ...

'If I have the sickness, there's nothing I can do about it,' she muttered to herself, repacking her fire-sticks and checking over her small campsite. It just means I have to find Luuka fast ... before it gets worse ... before ...

She swung the bag over her shoulder and scrambled onto the rocks, following their destructive path uphill to the top of the ridge. From there she had a good view over the surrounding forest. Deep shades of pine and spruce mixed with silver fir trees. Splashes of scarlet rowan and golden birch glowed in patches of pale sunshine. To the west, a line of granite cliffs split the forest like an angry scar. The river would be somewhere near the cliffs, she thought. The river, Boar Clan, Luuka. Her plans made, her direction set, she left the ridge and re-entered the dim forest.

The morning was well advanced by the time Kaija came to a small rivulet. It ran between mossy rocks to pool in the shade of over-hanging willows and ferns. With a thankful cry, she fell to her knees and cupped refreshing drafts of the cool, clear water. Her thirst quenched, she filled her water flask, then sat back against a rock.

She remembered the day she had made the flask. The hunt had been good, and as Clan Healer, Senja was entitled to a share of the kill. A young deer carcass was their portion, and Kaija had sat with her mother down by the river while they cut the tender meat into thin strips for drying and carefully washed the intestines, stomach and bladder. They would use these to store rendered fat and liquids. Nearby, a pot of succulent stew simmered in a leather cooking pot, rich with wood mushrooms and sorrel.

'Take the stomach as yours, Kaija,' her mother had said, handing it to the girl. 'And here is a leather thong to tie around the top. Now you have your own flask.'

Kaija ran her fingers over the rough leather thong and remembered how pleased she had been. It was quiet and still under the canopy of graceful willows and she closed her eyes, savouring the moment of peace and rest. Willowbark is good for fevers and headaches, she thought, intending to strip some of the fresh bark, but as she opened her eyes, her breath caught in her throat.

Crouched amongst the rocks and ferns was a lynx, and it was watching every move she made.

A New Friend

It was difficult to see the lynx in the dappled light. A prickle of fear crept down Kaija's spine and she sat, frozen, unsure what to do. She couldn't outrun it. If she moved suddenly, it would spring. But how long could she stay here? Already her legs were cramping under her. She moved one foot experimentally and the lynx bared its teeth, a snarl vibrating deep within its throat. Its tufted ears lay flat on its head and it lashed its tail from side to side.

So beautiful, Kaija thought. So deadly.

Without taking her eyes off the large cat, she felt behind her for a rock. Her other hand reached slowly for the leather sling tucked into her belt. She was accurate with her sling and often brought down squirrels or stoats or even a plump spotted woodcock, but she had never hunted anything as big as the lynx.

Her hands closed on a small, mossy rock, just as the

cat bunched its muscles and leapt towards her. Kaija had no time for the sling. She flung her rock and dived to the side. It flew wide and the angry cat landed lightly on its feet, ready to attack again, but, before it could, a short spear flew through the air and lanced the cat in the neck. It collapsed at her feet with a final snarl.

Kaija stared at the bloodied corpse and realised she was shaking. She had come so close to having her own throat ripped out. Her head was spinning and she tried to slow her breathing. She was vaguely aware of the sound of branches pushed aside, and shuffling footsteps, as the owner of the spear approached. She raised her eyes and stared at two feet wrapped in muddy leather wrappings, then higher, past short, bowed legs, a stocky torso, and upwards to a face dominated by heavy brow ridges, a large nose, and two gentle brown eyes that looked at her in concern. She caught her breath in surprise.

'Esi?' she murmured. 'You're one of the Esi?'

The boy nodded. He seemed unsure what to do, and shuffled back and forth. Finally, he pointed at the dead lynx and then at her. Kaija shook her head and frowned, not sure what he wanted. He shuffled forward and pushed the carcass towards her.

'Do I ... do I want it?' Kaija strained to understand. 'No! No, you can have it.' She pushed herself to her feet as her rescuer wrenched his spear from the side of the lynx. It was a handsome animal, but the sight of it made her sick. He was welcome to his kill.

'Th . . . thank you,' Kaija said. She studied the boy curiously. She had never been so close to one of the Forest-dwellers before. He was younger than she had first thought. The top of his flattened head came only as high as her shoulder, and despite his muscled arms and chest, he didn't have the powerful size of a full-grown man of the Esi. Kaija judged him to be the same age as her and Luuka, about twelve summers.

She chewed her lip thoughtfully. She had been warned about the savage Esi, who would attack without reason and tear her limbs from her body, but looking into the boy's shy brown eyes, she felt no threat.

He spoke to her – his words rough and jagged to her ears – and Kaija shook her head.

'I'm sorry. I don't speak your words. My brother knows some of your words. He learned them from a trader up-river . . . but he's not here.' Her voice trailed away and she shrugged helplessly.

The boy shook his head. Kaija tried again.

'Esi.' She pointed at him. Then she pointed at herself. 'Kaija.'

'Yi . . . yaaa?' His voice was deep and low.

'Kaija!' She nodded and smiled, and the boy smiled, too. 'Yorv,' he said, pounding his chest. 'Yaiya . . . Yorv.'

'Yorv? That's your name?' The boy looked confused and stepped away from her, and Kaija realised she had sounded too excited. She took a deep breath and spoke slower. 'Kaija thanks Yorv for saving her . . .' She pointed at them both and placed her hands over her heart. 'From the lynx . . .' She pointed to the lynx. 'Yorv take lynx. His kill.' She wasn't sure if he would understand, but the boy nodded. He hoisted the dead animal over his shoulders and nodded again.

'Yaiya,' he said, in his deep voice, before disappearing once more into the forest.

'Safe journey, Yorv.'

Kaija stood and looked after him. 'You have to be more careful,' she scolded herself. She picked her way over the rivulet and started following it downstream. 'You think you're a hunter? That lynx nearly had you for dinner.'

A twig snapping underfoot, a sudden silence, followed by the stealthy rustle of undergrowth.

Tarin froze. He pushed his hood away from his ears and listened. Branches of pine and birch danced gently in the breeze. A squirrel darted along a fallen log, fossicking for fallen nuts. From far above came the plaintive cry of a windhover as it floated on the air. But beneath these sounds of the arctic forest, Tarin caught a whisper of something more – the sound of cautious footsteps. Someone was following him.

His pace had been slow, even slower than he had anticipated, and the river that would lead him to Bison Clan still seemed a long way off. At first, he had followed the course of a rivulet, as it wound through a shallow gully. A few green larch and alder trees clung to the riverbank, protected from the desiccating winds by the steep sides, but soon, the ground rose, becoming rockier and harder to traverse, and Tarin slipped often on the uneven ground.

His mammoth hide boots, which had seemed so warm and sturdy back at camp, were already soaked, and the sense of freedom and lightness he had carried from Mammoth Camp gave way to the gnawing ache of loneliness and a constant ache in his leg.

And now – someone was tracking him.

With trembling fingers, he threw his tent over a low-lying branch and anchored it with rocks. Then he ducked beneath the branches of a gnarled willow tree, and waited.

He didn't have long to wait.

Tarin held his breath as the figure moved downhill towards him. In the growing shadows, it was impossible to see clearly, but Tarin knew immediately it wasn't his father or any of the other Mammoth Clan hunters. It was too small. And making too much noise.

Suddenly, a rotten tree trunk gave way beneath the tracker's feet, pitching him into a tangle of undergrowth. He cried out as he tried to extricate himself, lost his footing and came rolling downhill towards Tarin's camp.

Tarin launched himself from his hiding place with a roar, tackling the tracker around the waist as he fought to regain his balance. But he wasn't used to attacking, and the tracker fought back, pushing Tarin off and springing to his feet. Breathing hard, both boys stared at each other, their eyes wild and their faces smeared with dirt.

'Niko!' Tarin was the first to find his voice. He stared in disbelief at the younger boy. His hair was matted with leaves and twigs, his tunic and leggings plastered in mud. Scratches covered his face and he looked hungry and tired. 'What are you doing here?'

Niko scowled, still crouching and ready to attack.

'Nothing.' He stood up and wiped his nose with his arm, leaving behind a long smear of mud. His eyes were watchful.

'You followed me from camp!'

'No, I didn't!'

'You did!' Tarin's voice rose. 'You followed me! Why did you do that?'

'Why?' Niko shouted back at him. 'Because you're going to fail, Tarin. That's why. Miika says so. My mother says so. Even Jarkko and Tuuli say so –'

'That's not true!'

'It is. I've heard them talk. They think I'm sleeping, but I'm not. Everyone in camp knows you can't do this. They all know you're not going to return. You won't get to the mountain to give the Earth Mother the Offering. You won't even get to Bison Camp, because you're weak, and pathetic, and –'

'Aargh!' With a snarl, Tarin lunged towards the other boy and wrestled him to the ground. A red mist clouded his eyes and his heart felt as though it would break through his chest. He wanted to hit Niko – hit something – and he swung his fists wildly. Niko fought back, swinging his own fists. They were evenly matched, despite the difference in age, and they rolled around and around in the dirt.

Tarin managed to pin Niko down. He sat astride him and pummelled him, until Niko kicked out with his legs, twisting away from Tarin and pushing him facedown into the soft earth. Tarin swung his arm behind him, catching Niko on the nose. The younger boy cried out as warm blood spurted over his face. He lashed out with his foot, grinding Tarin's weak leg against a fallen tree. The pain was like a fire, shooting through Tarin's body. His head spun. He fought against the dark hole that threatened to engulf him, and wrapped his arms around Niko, like a bear.

Then the two boys were rolling, one on top of the other, crashing through undergrowth and tangled briars, through rushes and clumps of sedge grass, down the grassy bank to the water. With a thud, they landed on top of a sheet of ice that covered a small, still pool. For one breathless moment they lay there, stunned. But the ice was too thin to support their weight, and with a resounding crack it splintered beneath them, dunking the boys into frigid water.

The pool wasn't deep, but both boys were still thoroughly soaked. They heaved themselves out of the water and up onto the riverbank, then lay there, coughing up water and shivering.

'G . . . get d . . . dry.' Tarin's teeth chattered so much he could hardly speak. Niko didn't even try to answer. He staggered to his feet and followed Tarin back to his campsite.

'Th . . . th . . . this is it?' He stared at Tarin's small tent. 'This is your shelter?'

'And where's yours?' Tarin didn't bother to look at him. He hurriedly stripped off his soaked clothes – his *beaska*, tunic, leggings, undershirt and boots. Quickly, he rummaged in his pack for a spare reindeer hide and rubbed it vigorously over his frozen limbs. 'Here.' He tossed the hide and a spare fur wrap to Niko.

'I have my own spare fur,' Niko muttered. He flung it back at him and it caught him in the face. Tarin gritted his teeth and remained silent. He crawled into his tent and wrapped himself in his sleeping furs. They were softest fox fur, sewn together with sinew to form a warm cocoon, and soon his shivering subsided. He glanced up as Niko, wrapped in his own furs, crawled into the tent after him. Then he set about silently making a fire in the cramped space.

He made a ring of stones, placing the nest of tinder inside, and leaned close to strike the firestones. His hands trembled, and the sparks were weak. One or two landed on the tinder, but no matter how carefully Tarin blew the ember, he couldn't awaken the flame.

'You're doing it wrong.' Niko pulled his furs tightly around his shoulders. 'You have to blow it faster.'

'My father says you have to blow it gently.' Tarin frowned at him. He picked up the nest of fungus, but the ember had blown out.

'Well, Miika says it's better if you blow faster.' Niko hunched his shoulders and glared at Tarin.

Tarin pressed his lips together firmly and struck the stones again until three or four sparks landed in the tinder. He drew a deep breath and blew sharply on the ember. A shower of hot sparks and dried bark jumped out of the fire-pit, scorching his skin and blowing dust into his eyes.

'That was too strong,' said Niko.

'Then you try,' Tarin said with a snap. He rubbed his eyes and pushed the firestones towards the other boy.

Niko held the stones awkwardly, unsure what to do.

'Doesn't Miika say anything about how to strike the stones?' Tarin blinked the last of the dust from his eyes. Niko didn't answer, but took a stone in each hand and brought them down sharply on each other. The strong flint hit the softer pyrite with a crack, shattering the fragile nodule.

'What have you done?' Tarin shouted.

'I . . . I . . . didn't mean to.' Niko looked horrified, holding the broken pieces in his hand. 'I . . . I'm sorry.'

Tarin took the pieces from him. His journey had only just begun. He was cold, he was wet. Without fire, how would he survive the harsh conditions of the *tundar*, the great stretch of barren lands he would have to cross to reach the mountains? He tried to speak, but no words came to him. He just sat staring in disbelief at the crumbled rock.

Niko dropped his head onto his knees and closed his eyes.

'Tarin?' he whispered. Tarin raised his eyes and looked at the younger boy. He could see his own misery reflected in his eyes. 'Do you have anything to eat?' When Tarin remained silent, Niko continued. 'It's just that . . . I haven't eaten . . . anything . . .' His voice trailed off and he dropped his head once more.

Tarin roused himself and put aside the broken stones. He rummaged in his pack, bringing out the small packets of food. He had finished the dried reindeer strips the previous day, and the currants. Now, there were only the traveller's cakes.

'Your brother gave me these,' Tarin said, remembering Jarkko's kindness. It seemed so long ago that he was standing there on the riverbank, the cosy earth-lodges clustered on the terrace behind. He unwrapped one of the travelling cakes and passed it to Niko.

Niko nodded his thanks and took a small bite, then ravenously pushed the whole cake into his mouth. Tarin watched as he swallowed the food, then passed him another.

'Th . . . thank you.' Niko's voice was subdued.

Tarin broke one of the cakes in half and nibbled the edge. He had four cakes left. Enough for one, maybe, but not enough for two. How long until they reached Bison Camp?

The thought caught him unawares. Did that mean they were both continuing on? He should send Niko back to Mammoth Camp, but without shelter and food, and without dry clothes . . .

Tarin's thoughts trailed off. He wasn't sure what to do. He wished his father were here. But if Kalle had been with him, they would now be sitting warming themselves in front of a crackling fire, food in their bellies, and dry clothes on their backs. If Kalle had been with him, they would already be at Bison Camp.

Tarin groaned and let his head bow and his shoulders slump. Three days into his great journey, and already he was failing. Everyone was right. He would never make it to Great Mother's Mountain. He would never return home and see his family again. He would die somewhere out here, cold and alone, and because of him, his clan would also die.

The howl of a wolf in the distance made Tarin jump. His hand stole to the pendant at his neck and closed over the cool bone. He felt the marks of Owl under his fingers, and it gave him strength. The tension across his shoulders eased and he lay listening to the sounds of the night.

Tonight, maybe, he would have that dream where he was Owl, flying high above the plains. Maybe, flying so high, he would see the mountains.

A soft snore told him Niko was already asleep, the last few crumbs of traveller's cake still clinging to his mouth, his bare feet sticking out of his fur wrap.

Tarin eased out of his sleeping fur and threw it over both of them like a blanket, tucking it around their feet and up under their chins.

The wolf howled again, then the night fell silent.

A lone wolf, Tarin thought. Maybe a long way from home, just like me. Cold and hungry. Lost and alone.

But at least now, he thought, as he drifted on the edge of sleep . . . at least now . . . I'm no longer alone.

Disaster

Tarin and Niko awoke the next morning to a world white with frost. In low-lying hollows, morning mist softened bare branches and grey rock, and the pale sun reflected off icicles dripping from the trees. The ground crackled beneath Tarin's feet as he carefully picked his way down to the stream for an early morning drink.

'Today we should get as close to the river as we can,' he said as Niko joined him. 'Then tomorrow we can cross.'

'But that still gives us two days until we reach Bison Clan.' Niko rubbed the icy water over his face.

'Two days, at least.' A frown crossed Tarin's face. Two days ... and a river to cross. The knot of anxiety in his stomach tightened. He sat down on a fallen tree trunk, stuffing soft mammoth wool into his boots. It felt snug, and hardly damp at all.

'Do you have more wool?' Niko asked, scraping his *beaska*

against the rough bark of a pine tree to break the crust of ice. Their clothes were still damp from the previous day.

Tarin shook his head. 'Use sedge grass.' He frowned thoughtfully as the younger boy pulled at handfuls of the insulating grass, recalling something that had occurred to him in the dark hours of the night. Two days to reach Bison Clan, one pack between them, and more snow on the way. Tarin could feel it in the air, and in the way his leg ached.

'Niko, do you have any supplies?'

The boy didn't answer.

Two days, if nothing goes wrong ... two traveller's cakes each ...

Tarin's heart sank. The steppes and meadows were rich with bounty, but it took time to gather grains and dig for roots. And you had to know where to look. Old Mother had taught him how to find wild carrots and blackberry brambles, and mushrooms hiding beneath the autumn leaves, but as winter tightened its grip upon the land, food was becoming scarce.

'I don't need supplies.' Niko jutted his chin forward as though daring Tarin to argue with him. 'Miika told me what the hunters do. We can set traps for food, and eat roots and berries ... and you have the cakes my brother gave you.'

Tarin rubbed his face and ran his hands through his hair. 'It takes time to set traps, and now we have no fire to roast the meat. The leaves are already falling. There are no berries left.'

Niko scratched his nose and shrugged. He pulled on his mittens and hood. 'Then we dig roots and eat nuts –'

'Your hood is rabbit skin,' Tarin continued, feeling his frustration grow. 'When the snow starts falling, you will need a wolverine hood to stop the ice forming around your face.'

'Then we can hunt wolverine. You have a spear. If you can't throw it yourself, then give it to me.'

'That spear is part of the Offering.' Tarin's voice was sharp. 'We can't use it to hunt!'

'Why not? Old Father always says we have to use the gifts the Earth Mother gives to us – to show our appreciation.'

'This is different.' Tarin shouldered his pack. 'You have no snow-shoes. How can you cross the *tundar*? We have no fire –'

'Jarkko says the snow on the *tundar* is firmer than the snow in the forests, and we can cut strips of birch bark and tie it to our feet and slide through the snow. He says that's what the traders do when they travel to the northern clans.'

'And does Jarkko tell you how to make fire without a firestone?' Tarin knew he sounded angry, but lack of sleep and the constant worrying was taking a toll on his spirits.

'Jarkko says you can make fire the old way, rubbing wood

together,' Niko said as he started scrambling up the side of the gully. He looked back at Tarin and scratched his nose. 'You want me to carry the pack?'

Tarin pressed his lips together and shook his head. He hoisted the pack onto his back, staggered a little, and started to climb.

'There's no wood on the *tundar*,' he said. He paused as he reached the top of the gully to catch his breath.

Niko shrugged. 'You worry too much, Tarin.'

The boys stood and looked out over the wide plain before them. The sky was a clear, pale blue, but already, clouds were building to the north, promising snowfall before dark. Tarin raised his head and followed the flight of two black kites far above. They were tracking something moving down in the grasslands, probably a lemming or marmot, he thought, and he felt his empty stomach contract in hunger.

Far away on the horizon was a darker line of trees, marking the river and Two Rock Peak. They would have to bear north for a time, and try to cross the river at the Peak. It would take them longer that way, but the crossing would be easier. Tarin settled his pack more comfortably across his shoulders and started down the hill.

'But what about breakfast?' Niko called, hurrying down the slope after him. 'And why are you going that way? Miika says it's quicker to head south. We can cut out a whole loop of the river and cross about level with Bison Clan. That would save us a whole day!'

'My father says we need to cross at Two Rock Peak –'

'But Miika says –'

'I know what Miika says!' Tarin stopped so suddenly that Niko collided with him. Tarin wobbled as he steadied his footing.

Suddenly, Niko grabbed his arm and hissed. 'Tarin, give me your spear! Quickly!'

Tarin followed Niko's intent gaze, but saw nothing. Then a tuft of grass twitched. A steppe hamster, round with summer fat, was digging at the base of a tussock, unaware of the danger.

'You . . . you can't use the Offering!' Tarin gasped, holding the spear to his chest as though to protect it.

Niko snorted. 'I've seen you using it to help you walk.'

'Th . . . that's different.' Tarin's face turned red.

'No, it's not. Hurry up, Tarin!' Niko hissed in irritation, his eyes fixed on the hamster. 'If we starve to death, then the Offering doesn't matter, does it?'

Still Tarin hesitated. He knew Niko made sense, but he didn't feel right about using the gifts. 'We . . . we don't have fire to cook it –'

'Then I'll eat it raw!' Niko said with a growl. 'Quickly, Tarin. Give it to me now!' He reached for the spear and wrenched it out of Tarin's grip. At the same time, the hamster realised its danger. It squealed and dived into a stand of tall grass. Niko bellowed in rage and lunged after the frightened animal.

'Niko! Wait!' Tarin yelled, but the boy kept running, the spear clasped firmly in his hand. 'Niko!' Tarin ran his hand through his hair and snorted in irritation. But there was no answer. He paused, then followed Niko into the long grass.

The grass towered over his head, bleached and brittle now that the soft greenness of summer was over. Tarin heard Niko's shouts and his running feet. Then the grass closed over him, muffling sights and sounds. Hampered by his pack and his leg, Tarin felt as though the grass was pushing him backwards.

'Niko?' His voice fell flat, and the grass swayed above him. Sweat dotted Tarin's forehead. His chest felt as though a heavy weight was crushing him and he was having trouble breathing. He dropped to one knee and clasped the pendant at his throat.

Spirit of Owl . . . help me fly . . .

He raised his eyes upwards and tried to catch a glimpse of the sky, just to make sure it was still there. A breeze parted the tall grass, showing him a patch of blue. The two kites still wheeled and swooped above him. Tarin heard a muted shout, and he pushed onwards through the grass, nearly falling in relief as it gave way to scrubland and then short, tufted meadow grass. Niko was standing on top of a rocky outcrop, his arms raised, his head thrown back as he screamed up into the sky. Lying at the foot of the rock was the steppe hamster, blood running from a wound in its side.

'I did it! I killed the hamster!' Another bellow of triumph burst from him. 'I am a hunter!'

Tarin stared in surprise at the small, crumpled creature, then he reached forward and picked up his spear – the spear of the Offering. The shaft was still strong and straight, and the carvings still told their tale ... but the tip was shattered and the spear head missing.

'Niko ...'

'I am a hunter! I am a man!'

'Niko!' Tarin raised his voice sharply, cutting through Niko's cries of triumph. The boy stopped and looked down at Tarin in surprise. 'The spear! It's broken.' Tarin held the shaft up for Niko to see.

'It must have hit the rock after I skewered the hamster. Tarin, did you see? I did it. I made my first kill!' His eyes glowed.

'I saw,' Tarin said. 'I saw. But the spear – it's broken. Niko, where is the spear head? Where is Taavo's spear head?'

Niko frowned, confused for a moment. 'Well, it must be in the hamster.'

The two boys had just started towards the dead hamster, when there was a piercing cry from above. Like lethal black spears, the two kites plummeted downwards, talons outstretched. Tarin cried out and lunged for the hamster – for the spear head – but as his fingers closed around the blood-soaked fur, one of the deadly talons struck him across the face. Warm blood spilled from the gash into his eyes. Tarin lashed out with his fist, but the birds were experienced hunters. With the hamster clutched firmly in their grasp, they rose skywards, leaving Tarin lying in the dust, holding nothing more than a tuft of fur.

'No!'

Tarin searched the sky, but the birds were already small black specks on the horizon. He dropped his head and banged the ground with his fists. Taavo's spear head was gone! He pushed himself to his feet. He didn't look at Niko – he couldn't. He gripped the shaft of the spear grimly, feeling the familiar carvings. Mammoth for protection, Bison for thanks, and Cave Bear for strength. All these mighty totems, these mighty Spirit guides.

And yet they had been defeated – by a hamster and a bird.

How can I go to the Mountain now with no Offering to give? Tarin wondered. How can I face the Earth Mother and say: I have failed?

Blizzard

Two days' march to Bison Clan. Twice that to return home. Tarin stood undecided.

'My hamster!' Niko still stared into the sky, his empty hands hanging by his side.

Tarin felt numb. He opened his mouth to speak, but his voice stuck in his throat and he could only whisper, 'The Offering . . .'

'You still have the spear and the rest of the Offering.' Niko scowled at him. 'I've lost everything! That was my kill, and I didn't even get to eat the liver!'

Tarin stared at him mutely and Niko snorted in annoyance.

'Miika says you have to eat the liver of your kill. That's what the hunters do. They eat the liver while it's warm and it gives you the strength of the animal.'

Tarin felt his stomach shrivel. 'The strength of a hamster?'

Niko glared at him and turned away.

The rest of the Offering . . . Niko was right. Would the Earth Mother mind so much if she didn't receive the spear head? To return to Mammoth Clan would be certain failure. Tarin imagined his father's face . . . his mother's face . . . how they would feel if he gave up so easily.

The journey will not be easy . . . it was never meant to be. Tarin could almost hear Old Father say the words. To give up now would be a mistake.

'Tarin! I'm so hungry. Can't we have another travelling cake?'

'No!' Tarin dabbed at the blood still oozing from the wound on his face. 'We can't. We don't have . . . we just can't.' He swung his pack onto his back and turned to the north, angry tears stinging his eyes.

Two days. Two days to Bison Clan.

'But you're going the long way,' Niko wailed, hurrying after him.

Tarin didn't answer. He clenched his fists and steadfastly refused to listen to Niko's shouts.

The river, he thought. If they could just make it to the river. They could catch a fish, or dig for bulrush roots. Or even find a clutch of eggs. His mouth watered just thinking about food. And sedge roots. We should have dug for sedge and sweet flag back by the stream. It's too late now. We can still collect barley and rye . . . but then what?

Tarin tried to remember how his mother prepared the grain. She used wide woven baskets to thresh the grain from the husk before parching it in the sun. But the only time Tarin had tried to help, Miika had laughed to see him doing women's work. After that, Tarin would run away and hide when it was time to pick the grain.

Now he wished he had watched more closely. He rubbed his stomach, trying to quell the emptiness. Now, all he could do was put one foot in front of the other and keep walking towards the distant line of trees.

The first snowflakes fell mid-afternoon.

'We could still cut across those hills and reach the river this afternoon.' Niko stood by a small stream, his hands on his hips, his gaze surveying the rolling hills.

Tarin ignored him and broke one of the traveller's cakes in half. He passed a piece to Niko.

'When we get back to camp,' Niko continued, 'I'm going to eat mammoth stew and roast bison, and those hazelnut cakes Helvi makes. And fresh fish, and roasted pine nuts, and willow grouse stuffed with wood mushrooms – the big, fat kind.'

A reluctant smile stole over Tarin's face as he nibbled his

cake. 'Currants mixed with lingonberries, sweet strawberries and fresh clover . . .'

'*Giron* roasted in the ground.'

'Reindeer stew and beechnuts.'

'Roasted aurochs with sweetest thistle greens and blackberries.'

Both boys sighed as they finished their meagre meal.

'Tuuli makes the best sunflower and hazelnut mash,' Tarin said. 'She spreads it on little pollen dumplings she cooks on top of the stew.' He shifted his weight and rubbed his leg. He could feel his muscles growing stronger each day, but towards afternoon the familiar ache became almost unbearable. He wished he could heat some water to make a soothing tea.

'Let's keep moving,' Niko said. 'Are you ready? Let's go.'

Tarin looked upwards, studying the heavy clouds swirling and tumbling above them.

'Perhaps we should camp here,' he murmured.

'Maybe we can just follow this tributary to the river,' Niko said, sounding sulky. 'Come on, Tarin. The snow will stop soon, and I want to get warm and dry and have food in my belly.'

Tarin struggled to his feet and frowned. Niko was already fording the stream. He really had no choice but to follow him. The water was icy cold, but only reached knee high.

Tarin clenched his teeth as he followed Niko to the other side. He grasped handfuls of reeds and pulled himself out of the water, his feet shattering the ice that crusted around the riverbank.

'Niko! We can dig for sedge roots.'

'Later,' Niko called, his voice whipped away by the wind. Tarin frowned as he scanned the sky once more. Clouds were closing in fast. He shook his feet, aware of the chill seeping through his layers of wool. He hoped they didn't have too many more streams to cross.

His father had warned him about the streams crisscrossing the steppes. Soon the water would stop flowing, as ice covered the land. Even the big rivers couldn't hold back winter. For as many as six cycles of the moon they would sleep under the ice, waiting for the warm breath of spring to awaken them. Then they would become raging torrents, carrying melt water from the glaciers south to the inland sea. Tarin had never been so far, but like the rest of Mammoth Clan, he enjoyed hearing stories of trading missions and travels to faraway places.

Only last winter, Jarmo and Markku had journeyed as far north as the Great Ice, crossing glaciers in their path. And Matti, Kalle's brother, often told the story of his travels, south past the inland sea, to a land where it was always warm and the sun always shone. Tarin shook his head. He wasn't sure if he would like that. How do people live without the snow? he wondered.

A shout interrupted his thoughts. 'Slow one, hurry up.'

Tarin shifted the pack on his back and leaned into the wind. The snow was falling faster now, and thicker. It swirled around his feet in eddies and lay in thick drifts on the ground before him. The temperature dropped. The sky darkened and a blustery wind buffeted him. Tarin pulled his hood closer around his face, his nose and throat aching as he breathed in the bitter, frigid air.

'Niko! Wait!' Tarin bent his head to follow Niko's footprints, but already they were blurring, disappearing under a blanketing of heavy, wet snow.

A sudden blast of wind nearly knocked him off his feet. It flattened the grass and whipped the snow drifts back into the air, enveloping him in white. Tarin glanced at the sky, and felt his heart drop. The clouds were a swirling, ominous mass. A snowstorm . . . and they were unprepared.

'Tarin!'

He heard the call far off to his left and turned towards it.

'Niko!'

The wind whipped his voice away, driving icy needles into his exposed skin and sucking moisture from his lips. His feet and legs were numb, his wet leggings frozen. The pack on his back felt as though it contained rocks.

Time became meaningless. The afternoon deepened and they lost what little light there was. In the gloom, Tarin struggled onwards.

'Niko, wait for me!' he shouted into the wind. He felt as though he had been fighting against the storm for hours.

'Tarin!'

He heard Niko's desperate cry, and this time it was closer. A dark shape loomed before him, and suddenly he was grasping Niko's arms.

'We need shelter,' Tarin gasped. Niko was shaking so much he couldn't speak. Tarin looked around frantically, but the world was completely white. He tried to move forward, but floundered in a deep drift of snow.

Fear gripped him. Without shelter, they were in grave danger. Tarin had no idea which way to turn. He had lost all sense of direction. He spun around, desperately searching for some sign of shelter – a cave, a fallen tree – anything that would protect them from the driving winds and glacial cold.

A shrill cry pierced the wind. A flurry of wings and claws speared downwards, so close that Tarin felt the brush of softest feathers against his cheek. He yelled in fright, falling backwards, the image of fierce eyes burning in his mind as the large snowy owl swooped away. Tarin gasped for breath, each freezing mouthful searing his throat. He struggled to his feet. Through the flurry of snow, he saw a shape … a shadow. He staggered towards it, dragging Niko with him.

It wasn't a cave, it wasn't even a shelter, but in a blizzard it was enough. An embankment had caved away with the last spring rains, almost taking a birch tree with it. But the tenacious roots had clung desperately to the crumbling bank, forming a small overhang.

Tarin pushed Niko in first, before following him and dragging the pack behind them. With shaking fingers, he struggled to untie the wet leather thongs that held the pack together. He found the fox furs and wrapped them around them both, fur side in, followed by the reindeer hide. Then he took the aurochs hide tent and pulled it over them, tucking it under their frozen feet and over their heads. The darkness enveloped them, and slowly the boys stopped shivering.

Finally they slept, exhausted by their fight against the blizzard.

In Tarin's dreams, he was walking with Old Father to the top of the rise, where the grey granite stones rose towards the sky and cast their shadows over the rocky gorge. It was the day before he was to leave the Mammoth Clan.

'Tell me about the dreams,' Old Father said, narrowing

his eyes against the wind. He settled his back against one of the large, flat rocks and motioned for Tarin to do the same. Tarin sat hesitantly, and studied the Spirit Keeper out of the corner of his eye. His hair was as grey as the rocks, his body bent and twisted with age. The lines that carved his face were ancient, like the gullies gouged from the plains by the constant winds and shifting ice. And yet, the spirit that burned within his deep-set eyes was as bright as the sun.

'How did you know?' Tarin asked.

Old Father didn't answer straightaway. He plucked a downy feather caught in a crack in the rock and held it out to the wind. They watched it dance as the wind captured it and stole it away.

'This place, Tarin, is a wild place…a sacred place. Remember that.' He drew in a deep breath and closed his eyes. 'Spirit of Wind, Spirit of Ice – these are the Old Ones. The Ancient Spirits that formed our land. Before Mammoth and Bison. There are few left who remember such Spirits …'

Tarin frowned, unsure what he meant. He wanted to edge away, to return to the lodges where Taavo and Erik were knapping flint to be shaped into spear tips. He wanted to sit with them, to talk and laugh. To take pleasure in the work and the feel of the stone. But Old Father was continuing his story. Tarin hoped he would hurry up and finish.

'Before our ancestors found this rich hunting ground and decided to call it our own, there were others who walked here.'

Tarin looked down at the river and scratched his nose. He felt he should know what Old Father was talking about, but the meaning escaped him. If this were a test, then he had failed. Unless . . .

'Do you mean . . . the Esi?'

A smile softened the harsh lines on the old man's face. 'The Esi,' he said, sighing the word in reverence. 'The Old Ones, the Ancient Ones . . . also called by lesser names. The Hidden People, Short Necks, Flat Heads . . . animals.'

Tarin nodded. He had heard all those names. He had used many of them, too, with the other children of Mammoth Clan – when they would tolerate his presence. They would sit in a circle around the fire and snigger about the short, bowed legs and ugly, coarse faces of the Esi. They lived in caves, reeking of animal waste, the older children whispered, and wore rotting furs upon their backs. They spoke in grunts, and they would come in the night to steal sleeping children from their furs, carrying them away to their caves to gnaw on their bones.

Tarin had never seen the Esi. They had left the plains long before he was born.

'This was once their land,' Old Father said. 'Remember

that, Tarin. And remember the Old Spirits, who have walked this land since time began.'

'I will, Old Father.' Tarin frowned, puzzled. He didn't see what the Old Spirits and the Esi had to do with him or his dreams.

The Spirit Keeper's eyes gleamed. Tarin was a marmot caught in the gaze of an eagle.

'So polite, little owl,' Old Father said with a chuckle. 'Unlike others, who think they know better than an old man. But you listen, and learn, and you think. That is your strength. Yours is not the strength of the body. It is the strength of the heart and the mind. It is the strength of a Spirit Keeper.'

'I would rather be strong of body,' Tarin said. Dust made his eyes water.

'We do not always have the choice,' Old Father murmured. 'There are things we cannot control. We cannot control the wind. We cannot control the changing of the seasons, or the passage of the sun in the sky. And we cannot control the Spirits when they wish to talk to us.' Old Father looked down at Tarin. 'Dreams are the songs of the Old Spirits. It is how they speak to us. They bring us much knowledge, but they also bring fear and uncertainty.'

'I . . . I do not fear . . .' But Tarin's voice shook. Images crowded his mind. A dark cavern, stone walls wet and shining, a smell like rotting flesh . . .

'You will need protection on your journey.' Old Father's voice sliced through Tarin's memories and shattered them like shards of ice. He grasped Tarin's arm and pushed up his sleeve, exposing the soft flesh of his inner wrist. A blade flashed, sharpest flint, and Tarin felt a brief burning pain. Two curved lines marked his skin. His blood welled red against his white skin and dripped onto the grey rocks.

'Spirit of Owl, protect your child,' Old Father murmured. He held Tarin's wrist with one hand while the other reached into a pouch at his waist. He took a handful of bog moss and rubbed it into the wound. 'May his life blood return to the great Earth Mother.'

Tarin watched the last drops of his blood fall to the ground. With the next snow fall, it would wash away, to join with the water below. He held his arm against his body to soothe the pain. 'Old Father, will Owl guide me to the mountain?'

'Owl will guide you.' Old Father pushed himself to his feet, straightening with difficulty. 'And the Old Spirits. You will need their help to find the mountain. Spirit of Rock is strong in you.'

'And what will I do when I reach the mountain? How will I know where to go?'

'You will know.' Old Father took Tarin's arm, and clasped

his hand with surprising strength. 'You will know, because in your dreams, you have already been there.'

Yes, Tarin thought. In my dreams, I have been there. Darkness absolute. A long, twisting passage. The feeling of earth and rock pressing down, squeezing the air from his lungs . . .

Tarin woke up screaming.

The blizzard had blown itself out, leaving behind a soft covering of snow and the brilliant blue sky of a new day. Crisp, clean air filled Tarin's lungs as he squirmed out of the tangle of furs and twisted tree roots. He gulped it in, feeling his nightmare dissolve.

'Tarin, come and look at this!'

Niko stood on the top of the ridge, his arms spread wide and his face lifted to the rising sun. Tarin scrambled up the embankment to join him, and caught his breath at the panorama before them. Rolling hills, covered in crispest white, a band of deep green pines against the blazing blue sky, and in the distance, like a dark ribbon running through it all – the river, snaking its way southwards.

'We did it, Tarin!' Niko beamed at him and slapped him on the back. 'We did it. We made it to the river.'

Tarin shielded his eyes and studied the landscape. It was

the big river, but there was no sign of Two Rock Peak. He chewed his lip.

'Come on, Tarin. What are you waiting for?' Niko lifted his head and whooped for joy. Then he charged down the slope, slipping and sliding on the new cover of snow. Tarin followed more slowly.

During the blizzard, they must somehow have turned south, he thought. He could just make out a dark row of distant cliffs far to the north. To go that way now in the hope of finding Two Rock Peak would add days to their journey. Days they could ill afford.

He rubbed his head and tried to stop his thoughts from going round and round in circles. He felt a sudden pain and the cold, wet feeling of snow against his chest.

'Ha! Got you!' Niko gathered another handful of snow and hurled it towards him.

A wide grin broke out on Tarin's face and he hurriedly grabbed his own handful of snow and patted it into a ball. One of his fondest memories was playing in the snow with Taavo and his mother and father. He chuckled as he recalled a lucky snowball hitting his father. The sound of Kalle's booming laughter, and the sight of the big man with snow dripping from his beard and from his wild hair, pierced Tarin's heart and made him realise . . . he was a long way from home.

'Missed me,' Niko said with a laugh, as Tarin's snowball landed short. 'Come on, slow one. Today's the day we reach Bison Clan. I can feel it.'

A final tributary lay in their path, a swiftly flowing stream gathering melt water before joining with the great river. In spring it was a rushing torrent, carving a deep gully through the plains. In winter, when the great Ice Mother jealously guarded her glaciers, it flowed to a trickle, then stilled, locked in an icy prison.

'We'll have to go around,' said Tarin, standing at the lip of the gully. He studied the steep sides of grey rock. No trees grew, not even the small, tenacious spike moss could take root on the barren rock, and any that did were simply washed away in the spring floods.

'But we're so close,' Niko said. 'Half a day and we're there – at the river!'

Tarin chewed his lip. 'We have no choice.'

'You have no choice,' Niko said, anger darkening his brow. 'I could jump across the rocks, easily.'

'Then you do it,' Tarin snapped back. 'Because I cannot.' He turned away from Niko and dropped his pack on the ground. He lay down beside it and stretched out, staring up at the sky. Another obstacle. Disappointment stabbed him, but he pushed it aside. It would just take them a bit longer to reach the great river and Bison Clan.

The ache in his stomach was as constant as the ache in his leg. Tarin thought about the one cake they had left. They should wait until they absolutely needed it. But what if that was now? His stomach groaned and he pushed hard against it to stop the noise. He hesitated only a moment longer, then dug in his pack for the last cake. He broke it in half and handed a piece to Niko.

'Here,' he said. 'This is the last piece.'

Niko pressed his lips together in an angry line. Then he snatched the cake and shoved it into his mouth. He turned to walk away, but not before Tarin saw his eyes squeeze shut and a tear slip down his cheek.

Tarin hung his head. The steppe stretched around them in a never-ending sweep of grassland, giving no indication that they were even travelling in the right direction – and this was the easiest part of their journey. He shivered as he thought of the wild lands beyond Bison Clan.

'You can cross here, if you like,' Tarin said. 'I . . . I cannot. Even if I could get down into the gully, I'd never climb back out. But if you want to, we will meet again at Bison Camp.' He heard his voice waver as he spoke, and he clamped his lips together and swallowed hard, waiting for Niko to speak.

Niko shook his head, but didn't turn around. When he spoke, it was in such a low voice, Tarin had to move closer to hear him.

'If we die . . . it will be because of you, Tarin.'

Tarin hung his head even lower. He knew that. He told himself that all the time. But Niko was still speaking.

'Why you? Out of all Mammoth Clan – why did you have to be chosen to take the Offering?'

'I . . . I ruined the hunt. It is my task . . . my duty.' Tarin stumbled over his words.

Niko shook his head. 'But why not Taavo? Why not me?' As he spoke, his voice rose louder, until he was shouting at Tarin. 'You shouldn't even be alive. My mother says so. It should have been my brother who lived, not you.' With an angry sob, Niko turned from him and ran.

Tarin watched him go, feeling miserable. He started walking, but he had no strength, and his feet dragged along the ground. The pack was so heavy, his back bent with the weight and the muscles in his neck bunched into tight knots. Words swam around and around in his mind.

If we die, it will be because of you . . .

The boy is bad luck . . .

Tarin closed his eyes. Hot tears coursed down his cheeks. They stung the scratch on his face and left tracks in the dirt and grime.

It should have been my brother who lived, not you . . .

Tarin frowned. A story told to him many years ago hovered on the edge of remembrance. A story about a child born before Niko. He looked ahead to the small figure silhouetted against the sun. He may not understand Niko's words, but he understood the anger. He understood the need to run and run, as far as the hills would take you.

He just wasn't able to.

Washed Away

They reached the traveller's cairn as the sun dipped below the hills. Another night without reaching the river or Bison Clan, thought Tarin.

He had caught up with Niko by late afternoon, but neither of the boys spoke. They were tired and hungry, and lost in their own thoughts. They didn't even speak when the gully opened out and they were finally able to scramble across the stream.

The cairn was beside a small overhang. It was carved with the symbols of Bison Clan, with an arrow pointing towards the river. A mark cut below the waving lines, the symbol for river, told travellers how long the journey would take, but neither boy understood the counting words. Tarin scratched his head, but the vertical line with a small cross near the middle made no sense to him. He thought it shouldn't be too far, maybe a half day's walk.

Tarin had heard of the traveller's cairns – piles of rocks holding directions and emergency supplies. Clans would leave them on paths most travelled. Occasionally, they told of dangers or illnesses, especially those illnesses that spread quickly from person to person. Then the travellers would turn aside and take a different road.

Tarin and Niko quickly demolished the pile of rocks. Inside, was a small deer hide tent, the corner slightly chewed, wrapped around a stash of dried meat, cracked grains and a small woven basket containing dried fungus and shredded bark, kindling and a firestone.

'Food!' The word burst from Niko's lips.

'Wait!' Tarin grabbed Niko's hands.

'Why? It's food, Tarin. Food!' He pushed against the older boy, and Tarin toppled backwards, his hands grazing against hard rock.

'Don't do that!' Tarin pushed Niko back.

Niko snarled and lunged at Tarin, wrestling him to the ground. But both were weak from hunger, and they soon sat back on their haunches glowering at each other. A small trickle of blood ran from a cut near Niko's eye. 'I don't see why we can't eat it. That's what it's there for.' He scowled.

'We *can* eat it, but not so fast. It will make your stomach sick.' Tarin remembered a time when his father had returned from a long, lean journey. He had swallowed five bowls of reindeer stew before his stomach emptied it all back out again. Old Mother had laughed at him and said it was his own fault. When the stomach isn't used to food, too much can make you sick.

'And we can't eat it all. What if another traveller comes by?'

'We'll tell Bison Clan as soon as we arrive and they can restock it,' said Niko. 'Tarin, I'm starving!'

Tarin nodded. 'I am too.' Then he grinned, his eyes shining in anticipation. He held up the firestone and dried bark. 'Tomorrow, when we cross the river, we will get wet again. But tonight – we are going to have fire.'

'Fire!' Niko breathed the word reverently. 'We could dry our clothes.'

Tarin looked at the bountiful supplies before them, then grinned again. 'Here.' He passed Niko a strip of dried meat. 'Eat this while I build the fire.'

Tarin paused with the firestones in his hand, aware that Niko was secretly watching. What if I can't do it? he thought. What if I break the stones? Or the flame won't catch?

He shook his head to stop such thoughts. He had made fire before. There was no reason to think he couldn't do it again. He rolled his shoulders and tried to ease the ache in his muscles.

His first strike was a good one, and it drew a bright spark from the stones. Tarin quickly leaned forward and blew the spark gently.

'That's all wrong . . .' hissed Niko, waving his hands in the air.

Tarin turned his back on him and continued to blow. A red tongue flickered in the nest, eagerly devouring the dry tinder. Carefully he fed the rest of the kindling. Niko passed him some larger pieces of wood and Tarin set them around the flame, steeping the tips together to form a peak. The flame licked at them greedily and grew bigger.

'That's a good fire, Tarin.' Niko smiled as he held his hands out to the warmth.

Tarin nodded, too relieved to speak. He hovered anxiously over the flame. It seemed so fragile, protected only by the overhanging rocks. He was happier when they set the tent up and were able to remove their wet boots. He spread the mammoth wool and sedge grass out to dry, spread the reindeer hide on top and sat down, reaching white, wrinkled feet towards the warmth. Before long he had a small hide cooking pot suspended over the glowing embers. Meaty broth simmered gently, and by his side was a bone cup of willowbark tea.

'Tarin?' Niko's voice broke into his thoughts. 'That ravine. . . um . . . I couldn't have climbed down it either.'

A frown flickered over Tarin's face. He wanted to ask why Niko had been so angry. Why he had shouted at Tarin, and tried so hard to hurt him if he couldn't have climbed the gully either? But for the first time in days he was warm and dry and he had food in his belly. He shrugged the question away. It wasn't so important.

Tomorrow they would finally come to the river. A shadow passed over him and he shivered. For days, all they had thought about was getting to the river. They hadn't thought about what would happen when they did. How would they cross?

There must be a way, he thought, sipping his tea. The ache in his leg drifted away. Others have done it before. They could, too.

Night deepened. The fire danced and crackled, and somewhere in the forest an owl hooted.

He would worry about the crossing tomorrow.

Kaija scrambled across a fallen oak tree and followed a small stream as it flowed towards the larger river. Thickets of blackthorn, cherry trees and hazel brush caught in her hair and scratched her face, but following the rivulet became easier as the day went on. It became wider and the forest around it opened out, becoming less impenetrable. Instead of pushing through thickets, Kaija now walked freely over lichen-crusted rocks and soft leaves. Through stands of oak and hornbeam, she caught glimpses of roe deer and beavers, chattering squirrels and wild boars grubbing for roots, but she had no time to stop and hunt. Fear for her brother gripped her, and she hurried to make up time.

To the east, cloud heads were heavy with the threat of further snow. Despite the cool temperature, her constant moving had warmed her body and brought droplets of sweat to her brow. Snow would slow her down again, changing the landscape and leaving the ground icy. The seasons were changing, and Kaija didn't like the thought of spending winter alone and lost in the forest.

She munched thoughtfully on a handful of hazelnuts and late bilberries. How much longer would winter hold off? she wondered. What would she do then?

The thought chipped away at her constantly – shelter, food, water. She couldn't survive without them.

Kaija shook her head and stowed her flask. She picked up her pace until she was jogging. It kept her mind from worrying and her temperature from dropping. Soon, she would need to stop for the night – find a shelter and eat more food. She had to stay strong. The stomach cramps and headaches of yesterday hadn't returned, so hopefully it was just lack of food and water, and not the sickness that had made her feel so weak. Maybe Luuka's rabbits helped after all. The thought made her smile.

The ground was rockier now, and Kaija had to slow her pace. Her ankle still twinged on the uneven ground, but she drove herself as fast as she dared. By now, Boar Clan would have reached the river and turned south towards their home in the foothills of the cliffs. It was still a journey of many days.

Kaija rubbed her growling stomach and cast another glance at the sky. She should make it to the river before the snow started to fall.

The river was wide and turbulent, the churning depths cloudy with silt. Tarin studied the fast-flowing water and felt his stomach lurch. He could swim, of course. In the heat of summer, he liked nothing better than to float, weightless, in the river pools near home. In the water, he experienced a freedom he never could on land, but the sight of white peaked rapids and protruding rocks made him want to turn back the way they had come. Even Niko fell silent.

'How far can you swim?' Tarin asked, his eyes never leaving the churning water. A large tree branch floated by, swirling around as though it were no more than a leaf. It crashed against a rock and hung there for a moment, before the current picked it up and bore it away.

'I . . . I'm not sure,' said Niko, quietly. He repositioned the makeshift pack on his back – the pack made from the deer hide tent and carrying the last of the supplies from the traveller's cairn.

The boys were standing on the wide, rocky beach that led down to the water. Sheets of ice crusted along the quieter edges, freezing the sedge grass and reeds that grew in bogs and still ponds by the river's side. On the other side, steep grey cliffs rose almost vertically, studded with birch and alder and the occasional green pine. Tarin wondered how they were going to climb the cliffs.

'Jarkko says . . .' Niko swallowed, and fell silent. Then he tried again. 'Jarkko says, if you aim across the river and down. Don't fight against the current, but let it carry you.'

Tarin nodded feebly, but didn't answer.

'He says, keep your foot coverings and leggings on. They may get wet, but they are still some protection from the cold. He says . . . he says the water . . . is like . . . ice.'

'It is ice,' said Tarin, finding his voice. 'See the colour, that cloudy pale green? That means it's run-off from the glacier.'

He walked to the water's edge and scanned the far bank.

'We'll aim for that darker cliff over there,' he said, pointing a little downstream. Then he turned to Niko and clasped his shoulder. 'Keep kicking. Keep moving. Whatever you do, don't stop. We'll see each other on the other side.'

Niko pressed his lips together and nodded. His face was pale, but his gaze steady. Tarin hoped he looked as brave. They each re-tied the leather thongs around their leggings and mittens. Tarin checked his pack, tightening the straps. He slipped the spear shaft between two straps so his hands would be free to swim.

'See you on the other side,' said Niko, and started out into the water.

Tarin followed him, bracing his body against the cold. He gasped as the freezing water seeped into his boots and through his leggings. A sharp gust of wind drove icy needles into his face, tangling his hair and making his teeth chatter. He waded further, testing each step, feeling the rocks slip treacherously beneath his feet.

Other crossings had been as cold, but not so deep. Now his whole body was immersed in the glacial water. He felt the pack weigh him down, and for a moment he panicked, but as he moved further out into the channel, the water picked him up and swept him along.

Tarin soon realised they were going to overshoot the cliff on the other side. The current was stronger than he'd imagined, and unpredictable. Ahead of him, Niko's dark head bobbed up and down. Tarin kicked his legs and tried to move his arms, but they were growing numb. His legs felt heavy, as though he had rocks tied to them. His arms and shoulders ached, and he shivered uncontrollably.

White-tipped waves pounded him, filling his mouth with water and stinging his eyes. Branches and debris swirled in the current. A deer carcass, bloated and torn, floated by. Tarin avoided looking at the sightless eyes. He looked instead for Niko, but could no longer see him.

The river changed course and dark cliffs loomed overhead. Rocks emerged from the water, battering Tarin and sending him spinning. A tree branch speared him in the side and he gasped in pain. Water flooded his mouth and closed over his head.

He was sinking!

Tarin opened his eyes, but in the cloudy water he couldn't see anything. Spots swam before his eyes. The rocks on his arms and legs pulled him further under the water. He thought he should kick, but it seemed too much trouble.

Then the river picked him up again and smashed him against a broken tree trapped between two rocks. He grasped hold of the branches and, with a final effort, pulled his head up out of the water. He hung there, gasping for breath. He felt so tired. He wished he could close his eyes and sleep. He struggled to think. There was something he had to do first. What was it? It was something to do with the heavy rocks on his back. He wished he could get rid of the rocks. With one hand, he tugged at the leather thongs that held the pack on his back, but they were too wet to untie. His numb fingers fumbled with the knots before giving up.

If I could just close my eyes for a moment ...

Another branch crashed into the tangle of trapped debris, shaking his tree. He blinked in surprise to find himself still in the water.

The river! He was crossing the river.

He looked around for Niko, and his heart leapt as he saw another bedraggled figure caught in the twisted branches of the tree. The figure was limp and unmoving.

'Niko,' he shouted, but the figure didn't move. Slowly, Tarin pulled himself through the branches. He reached Niko and shook him. 'Niko, wake up! Niko!'

With fumbling fingers he tried to feel for a heartbeat, but his hands were too cold. Niko's face was pale and covered in scratches. He was missing one mitten, and his hand was icy cold.

'Niko! You have to wake up!' Tarin grabbed a handful of Niko's *beaska* and shook him as hard as he could. 'You have to, you have to, you have to.' He was screaming so loud, he almost missed the small groan from the half-drowned boy.

Niko's eyelids flickered and he licked his lips. 'S ... stop shaking me,' he murmured.

'Niko! You're alive!' Tarin shook him again. He looked around frantically. 'We're almost there, Niko. One more effort, and we've crossed the river.'

'I . . . I don't think I can, Tarin.' Niko closed his eyes again. 'I'm so tired. Just . . . let me . . . sleep . . .'

'No!' Tarin gripped the *beaska* and shook again. Niko's head wobbled, but he opened his eyes. 'We can do this. We have to.' Tarin reached up and snapped off part of the broken branch. 'Lean on this, and I'll help you.'

Niko nodded, and draped his arms over the branch.

'I can't carry you, or we'll both sink. But I'll be right behind you.' Tarin pushed them both back out into the flow of the river and kicked hard. He set his eyes on the bank and clenched his teeth. He had to succeed this time. He knew that. He would be too tired to try again.

At first he thought the shout was nothing more than a hallucination. But then it was repeated. He lifted his head and cried out. Men were on the far bank, beckoning to them, urging them on.

'Look, Niko! Help!' He saw Niko raise a weary head before collapsing back over the branch. Tarin forced his arms and legs to keep moving, to keep churning through the water, although they no longer felt a part of him.

Two of the men entered the water and swam out to meet them. Tarin had a brief glimpse of bearded faces, before a wave smacked him in the face. He coughed the water out of his screaming lungs and noticed Niko's branch sliding away.

'Kick, Niko,' he shouted, reaching out to push the branch closer to shore. They were close ... so close. But Tarin's strength was failing. He gave Niko's branch one final push towards the men. He could no longer move his legs and his arms were heavy weights. He felt the water engulf him in a gentle embrace. It lifted him up and away from the bank.

Somewhere, someone was shouting, but they seemed to be very far away. It was hard to hear them over the roaring in his ears. The water cradled him, sweeping him along, towards a narrow gorge. Tarin no longer felt the cold. He no longer shivered.

Tall granite cliffs forced the river to narrow. The current surged faster. Sheer rock rose either side, constraining the rushing torrent. Tarin was tumbled around and upside down. He couldn't see anything but the water and a blur of grey stone. The roar in his ears grew louder. The water turned white. He was through the gorge and falling. Over and over he tumbled. He hit the pool at the base of the waterfall with a suddenness that knocked all the breath from his body. Lights floated above him, sparkling in the green water even as he sank towards the dark depths.

Is this it? he wondered. Is this how I die?

He was only vaguely aware of the current once more

picking him up and carrying him further downstream. Slowly, the white water calmed. The stark grey cliffs softened, becoming more wooded and gently sloping. An owl soared high above, watching the river carry her prize southwards.

Tarin drifted in and out of consciousness. He didn't know when the river finally released her hold on him, tumbling him into the shallows. He didn't know when his feet first scraped against the rocks on the riverbed, or when his spear, still caught in his pack, wedged firmly between two rocks, trapping him there. He didn't know, because finally he had closed his eyes and slept.

In his dream, he followed the path downwards . . . always downwards, into chambers so dark he feared he would never see the light again. The air was heavy with the stench of dampness and rot. He felt his way along walls slick with moisture. There was no way out. No escape. The earth pressed against him . . . cold stone. It leeched the warmth from his bones. This is where I shall die. My bones shall lie here forever, never to be warm again.

But it didn't make sense. If he were destined to die far underground, he couldn't die here, by the side of the river. Tarin frowned. He opened his eyes to clear blue sky. He was still alive! For whatever reason, the Earth Mother had spared him.

Perhaps there is value in my life yet, he thought wearily.

Tarin had once asked Old Mother why the Earth Mother spared some lives and took others. It was after Ristak was gored by the bison. Tarin saw his body when the hunters carried him home. His wound was black with old blood and his stomach was hard as rock. He was bleeding inside, said Old Mother. She made her medicine, and Old Father sang to the Spirits. Tarin remembered the smell of the burning sage and the heavy smoke that curled around the top of the earth-lodge, seeking escape. Old Father said it was Ristak's spirit, looking to find its way home. While Taavo ran for Raisa and Erik, Tarin sat with the wounded man. He watched his chest rise painfully with each breath, and the blood bubble at the corners of his mouth.

Finally, he breathed no more.

'Why should Ristak die?' he asked Asa. 'The Earth Mother knows he is a great hunter.'

'Perhaps because she wishes him to hunt in the Spirit World,' said Old Mother. 'You should never question the Earth Mother's will, boy. She has a purpose for every one of her children.'

'Even me?'

Asa looked at him sternly. 'Even you. Especially you. Sometimes, the Earth Mother will make a choice. She will allow one of her children to live, and take another home to the Spirit World with her.' Old Mother stirred her pot of simmering herbs and her eyes looked into the shadows. 'There was another born the same year as you were, Tarin. The Earth Mother allowed you to live, as weak as you were, but in exchange she took the other child with her, to keep her company in the Spirit World. She must have a great purpose in mind for you, little Owl.'

Or perhaps she made a mistake, Tarin thought. Perhaps I was meant to die, and the other child – Maija's child, Niko's brother – was meant to live.

He closed his eyes and blocked out the sight of the sky and the sun. His lips were cracked and his tongue felt heavy. He couldn't move. Something pinned him to the rocks. He felt his blood begin to flow once more through his veins, like sharp splinters of flint. He began to shiver . . . and couldn't stop. Pain stabbed his fingers and toes. His body felt as though it were on fire.

Please, Earth Mother, take me with you to the Spirit World, Tarin begged.

A shadow fell across his face and he opened swollen eyes. Through parched lips, he whispered soundlessly . . .

Thank you.

For the Earth Mother had heard him, and she had come to take him home.

A Meeting
of Ways

At first, she thought it was a dead animal caught in the tangle of branches. Kaija picked her way carefully over the rocky bank. The first few flakes of snow were starting to fall. Driven by a glacial wind, they became icy needles, stinging her face and making her nose run, but curiosity drove her to have a closer look at the bedraggled body.

Not a dead animal, she decided. A dead boy. She picked up a large stick and poked him with it. He gave a faint moan, and she jumped back in surprise. A loose rock wobbled beneath her feet and Kaija sat down abruptly in an icy pool of water. She cried out in disgust as the water seeped through her leggings, but then the body moved, and she realised the boy was still alive – barely. A pale hand reached out to her, and for one irrational moment Kaija's heart leapt into her mouth. 'Retu!'

Even as the strangled cry left her lips, she knew this boy wasn't her brother. It may be kinder to let the river have him, she told herself. But she couldn't do that. Not while he lived. She would give him the chance that Retu never had. She clenched her teeth and waded into the icy water towards the tangled branches.

The boy was small, but his furs were heavy with water and Kaija struggled to disentangle him with shaking hands. 'Please be alive,' she muttered.

His eyelids fluttered, and for a moment he looked up at her, before his eyes rolled back and his head fell forward.

'No! Stay awake!' Kaija shook his thin shoulders, but the boy didn't respond.

A spear in his backpack wedged him firmly between two rocks and his head was in danger of slipping under the water. Rocks rolled under Kaija's feet as she tried to dislodge the spear. With a crack, it split in two.

Kaija hooked her arms around the boy and dragged him clear of the water and onto the rocky shore. She dragged her mitten off and tried to feel for a heartbeat, but her hand was icy cold and numb. The snow was falling faster now, blurring her vision. She looked around for shelter. Small caves littered the cliffs, but how would she get him there?

She breathed deeply and pushed her hair out of her eyes.

Her hand clasped the pendant at her neck and she whispered: 'Spirit of Horse, help me find the strength.' She closed her eyes briefly, then hooked her arms around his chest and dragged the unconscious boy towards a small cave above the water line.

The roof of the cave was low, forcing Kaija to turn and roll the boy into the dry interior. She laid him on his side and tried to feel for his breath. It was shallow, but he was breathing. She removed his backpack, struggling with the swollen knots, and stripped him of his sodden fur *beaska*. The soft buckskin tunic and fur jerkin underneath were also wet. Kaija rubbed his limbs, willing the warmth to return to him. She avoided touching the slashes on his wrist. They looked like a totem mark, but they were fresh and there was no black ochre that was usually used to make the tattoos. His face was still pale, but the blue tinge had left his lips.

Kaija shivered as she struggled to light a fire. Her arms felt heavy and her hands were trembling so much the sticks kept slipping. Finally, she threw the sticks down and sat with her head on her knees. Exhaustion overwhelmed her. Her chest and throat ached. She squeezed her eyes shut and dug her palms into them to stop the tears that threatened to fall.

Less than seven nights ago, she thought, her life had been normal. Retu was alive, she hadn't lost Luuka, and they had had food to eat and warm dry furs to wear.

'I want to go home.' The words burst from her lips. She forced herself to take deep breaths, holding each one and trying to calm herself. Slowly, her tears stopped and she considered her situation.

She couldn't go home, that was certain. The sickness would still be there. Images of pale, gaunt faces with fever-red eyes washed over her, and her mother's anguished cry: 'Not the boy! Don't take my son from me –'

'No, no . . . don't think about it . . .' she muttered, rubbing her forehead.

And what about Luuka? She couldn't go home without him and lose another brother. She looked down at the sleeping boy. The resemblance to Retu was still there, but he wasn't as fair. His long, tangled hair was brown and when he had opened his eyes back in the river, they were grey. It was only his small size that made her think he was her brother.

Giving into her exhaustion, Kaija lay down next to the boy. She wrapped her arms around him, and slowly her shaking subsided. Some warmth crept into her icy body, and Kaija closed her eyes and slept.

A frantic cry and thrashing limbs woke Kaija. The boy was unconscious, but he tossed and turned. His eyes were open, but Kaija knew he didn't see her. His mind was tortured by the fever wracking his body. She touched his forehead, and it felt as though a flame were burning beneath his skin. As the daughter of a healer, Kaija knew the battle his body was waging. She wished she had stopped to cut the willowbark, but it was too late now.

She spoke in a low, calm voice to the boy, and some of her words must have penetrated his fevered mind, because he stopped fighting her and lay still again, moaning. He sounded just like her brother when the sickness ravaged him, and Kaija felt her heart clench.

'Shh, shh, shh . . .' she murmured, crooning softly, brushing the damp hair off his forehead.

'M . . . mother?' The boy's voice was little more than a tortured whisper.

'Shh, rest now,' she said, and the boy seemed happy to lie still. But his breathing was laboured and his body shook with fever.

'What do I do? What do I do?' Kaija tried to think back to the lessons her mother had taught her.

'Kaija, pay attention,' her mother would say, dragging her through the meadow. 'This is elecampane. See the yellow flowers? Now dig down to the roots . . .'

Kaija sat in the dark cave and stared into the shadows. She hadn't been interested in learning about the herbs.

She didn't want to be a healer. She wanted to hunt or make furs or work the flint ... She sniffed and rubbed her nose. Well, she may not remember the hundreds of herbs in Senja's medicine bags, but there was one thing she could do – she could make fire and keep them warm.

She felt for her fire-sticks – the drill and the softer platform. They were still lying where she had thrown them some hours ago, along with the dried fungus and bulrush fuzz she used as tinder.

Kaija had been lighting fires since she was a small girl, and she often did so in the middle of the night, when her mother would be called from their soft, warm sleeping furs to heal a patient – to set a broken bone, or cool a fever, or even birth a baby.

She knew, just by the feel of the sticks, how to position them, and with a firm downward pressure she started spinning the drill into the platform. Her hands were steadier now, and her muscles rested, and it didn't take long for her to scent the first faint trace of wood smoke. An ember glowed in the darkness, like a tiny star in the night sky. Kaija leaned close and blew the flame to life, enjoying now, as always, the feeling of creating the flame from nothing.

She turned her attention to the boy. His face was flushed and sweat beaded his forehead. She moistened his dry lips with the water from her flask and he licked it greedily. His eyes opened once more. Grey as the feathers of the Great Grey Owls that lived in the high reaches of the forest.

'Water,' he moaned.

Kaija held his head and dribbled some water into his mouth. The effort exhausted the boy, because his eyes fluttered again and he lay back.

'I wish I could help you,' Kaija whispered. She was no longer sleepy and sat watching her patient. His backpack lay where she had left it. It was nearly as large as he was and well made. Kaija chewed her fingernail. She didn't like opening it without the boy's knowledge, but it might contain something that would help him – food or dry furs. Food would help her, too. Her meagre meal of hazelnuts and berries was a long time ago, and her stomach growled angrily. She clasped her pendant and sent a silent plea to her totem guide to help her do the right thing.

'Forgive me,' Kaija whispered to the unconscious boy, as she untied the straps holding the pack together. She pulled the aurochs hide tent and reindeer skin from the pack, followed by the fox furs. The boy's tunic was wet with his sweat, his movements agitated, but as Kaija wrapped the fox furs around him, he calmed and breathed more easily.

Water had ruined a small birch bark box containing a stone and some soggy bark, but his bone cup was undamaged. In the bottom of his pack, wrapped carefully in a snow leopard fur, was a small bundle. Kaija paused before unwrapping it, her fingers digging deep into the luxurious fur. She glanced at the sleeping boy. In the flickering firelight, he seemed smaller than ever. Dark circles bruised the skin beneath his eyes.

Curiosity won, and she untied the leather thongs securing the bundle. A gasp escaped her as she examined the contents. Finest buckskin leather, a flint blade, a large tooth – Kaija examined it closely and decided it was a cave bear tooth. Two carved ivory beads and a small piece of amber.

She lifted her gaze from the precious items laid out in front of her and looked at the boy.

'Who are you?' she whispered, frowning. 'And why do you carry such riches?'

The boy groaned and stirred in his sleep. Kaija returned her attention to the parcel. She felt her pulse quicken as she examined the last two items. With shaking fingers she unlaced the leather thong holding a grass-wrapped packet together.

Food! Kaija cried out in disbelief. Strips of dried reindeer and smaller packets of dried berries – crowberries, raspberries and sweet yellow cloudberries. Sweet rush roots and milk vetch pods, cracked grains of rye and beechnuts. And traveller's cakes of rich, mouth-watering fat mixed with berries, grains and a deep, pink meat Kaija thought might be salmon. She felt her stomach cramp just looking at the feast before her.

We're saved.

Kaija closed her eyes and clasped her pendant. Her head spun and she felt as though she couldn't breathe. She glanced guiltily at the boy as she took one of the cakes and bit into it. Tears came to her eyes, and she forced herself to chew slowly and swallow a small bit at a time.

'I'm sorry,' she whispered. 'But I need this food. I'll pay you back, I promise. I'll hunt, and find berries and mushrooms . . . I promise I will.'

She finished the cake and looked longingly at the rest, but she also knew her shrunken stomach would only hold a little bit at a time. Reluctantly, she placed the rest of the food aside and turned to the final item.

All that remained now in the snow leopard skin was a fur pouch. Kaija took a deep breath and studied the pouch. It reminded her of the one her mother carried, made of deer's stomach and covered with ermine. This one was white, too, but it was reindeer. Inside were smaller packets of dried herbs and powdered roots. Medicine!

Kaija sorted through the small packets. She recognised the scent of camomile and wood sorrel, meadow sweet and willowbark.

Kaija, pay attention . . .

Her mother's words came back to her. Camomile to soothe the stomach. Yellow-flowered coltsfoot to calm the most persistent cough. To strengthen the blood, take a tea of stinging nettle and hawthorn, and willowbark . . . Kaija smiled as she smelled the familiar herb. 'Willowbark tea for almost anything,' she murmured. 'But especially for fever and aches.'

But how could she heat the water? Kaija looked around at their meagre supplies in frustration. She and Luuka had fled their camp so hurriedly they had brought nothing with them. It was growing light outside, and she stared out of the cave towards the river.

'We have plenty of water,' she murmured. 'And now we have fire. But I need a pot to heat the water.' She picked up the reindeer hide and ran it through her fingers. It would have to do. She could use one of the leather thongs to lash it to a wooden frame; there were plenty of rocks in the river to use to heat the water; and they could share the boy's cup.

Kaija grabbed her water flask and crawled out of the cave, eager now to put her plans into action.

A New Plan

Morning mist covered the riverbanks, and the slippery ground was treacherous. Kaija picked her way carefully across the stones to a small pool. During the night, a cover of ice had formed over the surface. She broke it into shards before splashing her face with the bracing water. Smooth round pebbles, a full water flask, an assortment of tangled driftwood, and she was ready to return to the cave.

The boy was still sleeping when she returned, but his sleep was disturbed and his forehead creased with pain. He called out names of people Kaija didn't know – mother and father, she recognised, but he also called other names like Niko and Taavo. He was especially anxious about Niko. Kaija wondered if his camp had suffered the sickness as well, which would explain why he was alone in the forest with such unusual cargo.

She cut a thin leather strip and a larger circular shape

from the reindeer hide, and using her flint knife, she poked small holes around the edge. Then, with a sharpened stick, she pushed the leather thong through the holes, lashing the hide to a frame of driftwood. Kaija filled it with water from her flask and suspended it above the fire, careful not to let the bottom of the pot get too close to the flames.

While she was busy making her pot, she placed the rounded river stones in the fire and let them heat. She slipped one of her mittens back on. Using a stick to drag a heated rock from the fire, she picked it up and dumped it into the water. The water hissed and steam rose as the heat from the rock passed to the water. Then another rock heated the water a little bit more . . . and another . . .

Soon the water was hot, and Kaija tossed a handful of willowbark and camomile into it. The scent was familiar, and comforting. She shook the boy's shoulder, waking him enough to take some small sips of tea. It seemed to comfort him, too, because he slept more soundly then, and when Kaija placed her hand against his forehead, he felt cooler.

Maybe I am a healer, Kaija thought, smoothing the furs around her patient. I hope I make a better healer than I do a hunter or tracker. Boar Clan were far ahead of her now, and the thought saddened her.

Luuka, I'm sorry. But you know I can't leave . . . not yet. She looked down at her patient. *He'll die if I leave now. Maybe he'll wake soon, and then I can try and follow you.*

But the boy slept all day and into the night. Kaija kept waking him, giving him sips of the tea whenever he became restless. His fever came and went, and seemed to grow worse towards nightfall.

'It's so dark,' he cried out once, sitting up abruptly and hitting his head on the rocky roof of the cave. 'I don't want to die!' His eyes were like pools of misery in a pale, pinched face, and he shouted deliriously.

'Shh . . . you won't die,' Kaija murmured. She tried to place one of the buckskin strips on his forehead. She had soaked it in sweet-smelling camomile, but he fought with her as she tried to calm him and wouldn't lie still. His body was bathed in sweat, and Kaija feared the illness which raged inside him was too great for her to heal. When his flailing arms knocked the pot of tea over the fire, quenching the flames, Kaija screamed at him and crouched in a corner of the cave, sobs shaking her body. She was beyond exhaustion.

But sometime in the early hours of the morning, the boy's fever broke.

As the first light of dawn crept into the cave, Tarin opened blurry eyes and looked about him. He was puzzled, first by the cave, and then by the girl sleeping next to him. Tousled hair covered her face – hair so fair it was almost white. Did he dream of her once? He felt he had seen her before. She looked cold, lying there on the floor of the cave. Tarin took his fox furs and spread them over her, tucking them around her feet. She murmured in her sleep.

'Retu?' Her voice was puzzled . . . groggy. She opened her eyes and stared unseeing in front of her.

'Shhh . . .' Tarin murmured. 'Sleep now.' He watched as the girl closed her eyes and her breathing slowed. Then he, too, closed his eyes and slept.

Kaija woke the next morning to a world renewed. In a last show of strength before winter took hold, the sun beat down with unseasonable warmth. Kaija stretched her arms above her head as she came out of the cave and looked around in pleasure. The autumn forest shone burnished gold and red, and high above, clouds scurried frantically across a blue sky.

Today – she promised herself as she broke through a sheet of ice to reach the water beneath – today, she would continue her quest to find her brother. She sat back on her heels and watched the sparkling water cascade over the rocks. But she couldn't stay idle for long. She needed to build a new fire, heat some water for tea, maybe she could even cook something . . . Kaija jumped to her feet, feeling full of energy, and hurried back to the cave.

The boy was still sleeping, but his sleep was peaceful and he was free of the fever that had ravaged him. Careful not to disturb him, Kaija picked up the pile of clothing that lay in a tangled bundle at his feet. She spread the damp coats and furs over rocks and branches to dry. Their boots, too, needed drying, and she carefully spread the inner lining of felted wool in a patch of sunlight. She studied the boy's clothes as she laid them out.

They were similar to her own, but plainer. Feathers, shells and beads covered Kaija's tunic, but his was bare of any decoration: tunic and leggings of soft buckskin laced together with sinew; outer trousers of fur, flapped over in front and tied with a drawstring; boots made of thick hide, also worn laced and tied over the legs; a rabbit-skin jerkin; an outer wrapping of reindeer; an inner hood of wolverine; and the heavy, hooded *beaska*. Kaija stroked the coarse brown fur thoughtfully.

'Mammoth!' she whispered, recognising the thick, wiry fur. She glanced across to the mouth of the cave where the boy lay sleeping. 'Either your clan has traded well with the Mammutti, or you're a long way from home.'

She left the clothes to air while she moved her cooking

fire outside the cave. Soon, a pot of broth was simmering. The smell was tantalising, and her mouth watered at the thought of food, but Kaija satisfied herself with a small strip of dried meat. She would wait for the boy to wake, then they would both share the broth.

As Kaija sat and munched the meat, she took further stock of her surroundings. The cliff opposite her rose steeply towards the sky, but through the trees she thought she could make out a rocky path. She frowned in concentration and her gaze followed the path back down to the river. But then where did it go? The river was flowing too fast to afford a safe crossing. She narrowed her eyes and scanned the opposite bank. A faint break in the tree line followed the river upstream.

Kaija glanced towards the cave, and then at her cooking pot. The boy was still sleeping and her broth was already cooked. She moved the pot away from the fire and decided to explore upstream. It had been close on dark when she first came to the river, and then the snow and the boy had stopped her going any further. If there was a path . . . Kaija gasped aloud as a thrill surged through her veins. She hurried onwards. If there was a path, then there would be a camp. And if a camp was close by, it could be Boar Clan.

She started to shake in excitement, missed her footing amongst the rocks and fell, scraping her knee. The pain made her slow down and tread more carefully.

But if it was a Boar Clan path, then how did they get across the river? Kaija's clan used rafts made of alder trees to cross the river near her home. But there, the water was wide and slow. She had also seen the dugout boats used by the Second Cave of River Clan. They would fell full-grown trees and dig the centre from the wood. But the water here was white, warning of hidden rocks and great danger.

Kaija rounded the bend in the river, and found the answer to her question.

Sometime recently, a huge pine tree had lost its grip on the rocky cliff and fallen across the gorge, its great expanse reaching to the far shore. The water still surged beneath it, but the tree formed a perfect bridge from one side of the river to the other. Boar Clan simply had to cut the branches from the trunk to cross the river easily and extend their territory.

The tree trunk was slippery, but Kaija was sure-footed. She reached the other side of the river and followed the narrow rocky path as it wound upwards. The drop to the river was precarious, and Kaija pressed herself against the rock wall. Far below her, she could hear the rush of water. At the top of the cliff she paused, and caught her breath at the beauty before her. The forest canopy was an undulating sea of deep green and autumn splendour. Far below, the river boiled, squeezed on both sides by sheer granite. From where she was, Kaija had a clear view of her camp – her cooking fire and the clothes left to dry. She suddenly felt very vulnerable.

Her gaze followed the course of the river downstream. Here, the cliffs softened, the narrow chasm opening out to rolling hills. The river widened, the white water calmed, and still the forest stretched endlessly to the distant horizon.

A thin plume of smoke near a bend in the river caught her attention. Kaija narrowed her eyes, shielding them from the sun. People were camped down there! She stepped back into the cover of the trees. If she could see them, then they could see her, standing out on the edge of the cliff. She watched the plume of smoke, and gradually more detail became clear – small huts by the side of the river and people moving. How close she had been! Imagine if they had seen her own fire's smoke. Kaija clutched her pendant and closed her eyes.

'Spirit of Horse, and Spirit of Snow, I thank you for keeping us safe and hidden while the boy was ill.' She paused and opened her eyes. 'But now I ask for more help – that I can get closer to the camp without being seen.'

Slowly, Kaija edged down the path towards the camp. She was too far away to tell if it was Boar Clan, but in her heart, she felt that it was. She set her feet carefully, so no stray rock would give her away, and she paused periodically to watch the movements around the camp. But no alarm was raised, and no angry hunters came rushing towards her.

Once she reached the bottom of the cliff path, she moved more quickly. The deep carpet of fallen leaves muffled the sound of her feet, and she leapt nimbly over fallen tree trunks and mossy boulders. A small clearing on a rise above the camp gave her a perfect vantage point. She swung herself up into the boughs of a massive pine tree, scratching her arms and legs on the rough bark, and studied the scene below.

Half a dozen huts clustered on a flat terrace above the river. They were circular, made from a large central wooden pole and covered with hides. A pair of boar tusks hung above each doorway. Kaija caught her breath. She had found Boar Camp! She was so excited, she leaned forward, nearly falling out of her tree.

A leather flap covering the doorway of the largest hut flung open, and Kaija shrank back into the leaves. The tall man that stood there, stretching his arms and scratching his belly, was one of the hunters who had chased her and Luuka. She was sure of it. She watched him swagger towards a small lean-to made of twisted branches and speak to the two men standing either side of it.

Guards! Kaija chewed her lip in agitation. Surely that

was where they were holding Luuka – and that meant he was still alive! She gripped the branch of her tree so hard the rough pine bark stabbed her skin. Her first impulse was to rush forward, but she forced herself to sit still and watch.

The hunter was laughing with the guards. He dropped his trousers and relieved himself on the side of the hut as the guards dragged their prisoner from it.

'Luuka!' Her brother's name escaped her lips, and Kaija had to clench her teeth together to stop from crying out. He was alive, but bloodied and pale. His two guards threw him to the ground and he lay there, unmoving. The guards picked him up by the ankles and dragged him down to the river.

Kaija crouched, ready to spring to her brother's rescue if they tried to drown him, but the men just dunked his head into the water and dragged him back towards the central cooking fire, still laughing. They threw him in the mud near a girl tending a cooking pot. She shuffled away from him and wiped her nose with the back of her sleeve. An older woman shouted at the laughing men and waved them away. She cuffed the girl around the ear and squatted before Luuka.

She brushed tangled hair off his face and held his chin. She spooned liquid into his mouth, but it made him choke and cough. Most of the liquid ran out of his mouth and down his chest. Kaija had seen enough. She sat back in the branches and wiped her eyes savagely. She had been unaware of the tears flowing down her cheeks.

She had to rescue her brother, but she had to have a plan. Maybe when it's dark, she thought. She could slip into the camp and release him. But in his weakened condition, how could he run? And how could she get him out of his prison? Kaija leaned her head against her knees. She needed help.

She thought of the boy back at the beach camp. There was no one else. And she wouldn't give in. While Luuka was alive, there was hope.

She raised her head and studied the camp again, noting every hut, planning for her return. The girl had finished her cooking and was now rinsing her pots down by the river. A couple of coracles, small boats made of willow and animal hide, bobbed on the river. Nets made of twisted hair hung drying on posts. A row of short, squat spears lay unfinished by the fire.

Kaija nodded thoughtfully, climbed down from her tree and made her way back over the cliff, plans whirling in her head.

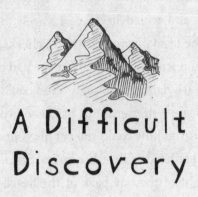

A Difficult Discovery

Tarin opened one bleary eye and looked around. The cave was small, hardly more than a hole, but it felt familiar. Grey rock walls, low ceiling. He looked thoughtfully at the remains of a small fire pit. The ashes were grey and cold.

He pulled at the fur around his shoulders and tried to sit up. His mother's snow leopard skin. There were things here that didn't make sense, but when he tried to think, the walls of the cave blurred and wavered. He lay down again and waited for his head to stop spinning.

Memories crowded him – chaotic, jumbled images.

Niko, pale and cold . . . lifeless. Tarin frowned, unsure of what he had seen and what he had dreamed. Had there truly been a man wading towards Niko, gathering him in his arms and throwing him over his shoulder?

And then the pain. Was that also just a dream? The ice-breath of Mother Winter that froze his heart and turned the blood in his veins to frost as he was tumbled like a river stone in the embrace of a raging current.

But then she'd come – the Earth Mother. Her hair the colour of snow, her eyes the colour of sky. She'd given him warmth, and he'd cried out as the fire returned to his body, chasing the frost and melting the ice in his veins.

I am alive because of the Earth Mother.

And yet . . . there was also a girl in his dreams. She gave him water to wet his parched lips, and her voice was like a song.

As he lay there and tried to follow the fleeting memories, a figure appeared at the entrance of the cave, a dark shadow against the bright sun.

'You're awake!'

It seemed a stupid thing to say, but Tarin nodded his head. It didn't spin so much this time, so he tried to sit up. The girl hurried to his side and held a fur-covered flask to his lips. It was the sweetest water he had ever tasted, and icy cold. Her fair hair hung over her face and she frowned as she felt his forehead. Her lips moved, but a fog still sur-rounded Tarin's brain, and he couldn't hear her words. He shook his head and suddenly sound rushed in upon him.

' . . . broth of dried meat and grains.'

The words sounded good. Tarin nodded weakly.

The girl left him with the water flask and hurried out of the cave. Slowly, Tarin followed. His legs felt as though they were made of water and he grabbed the rocky cave walls to stop from falling. Sunlight beckoned.

At first, the light was too bright for his eyes, but then shapes and shadows formed themselves into solid trees – spruce and alder – and rocky cliffs. Tarin moved further out of the cave and sat on a rock. His legs shook with the effort but he looked around in interest.

He was on a rocky beach beside the swiftly flowing river, surrounded by grey cliffs. Pine and scarlet rowan reached for the sky, their roots clasping grimly to the sheer rock. Far above, a bird soared, gliding on the wind. Tarin shaded his eyes to watch its graceful flight and thought it might be an eagle, hunting, its keen eyes trained on the forest below. With breathtaking speed, the eagle plummeted earthwards to swoop on its prey. Tarin's belly grumbled at the thought of food.

He turned his attention back to the beach. It was strewn with driftwood and bleached bones, debris forced through the cataract of cliffs . . . just like he was. Tarin picked up a grey stone and hefted it in his hands. Flint! And there, lying along the shore, were fire stones, cast up by the surging water. He could replenish his stock before leaving.

The thought sobered Tarin. He must continue his quest . . . but . . . where was he? He had been taken by the river – but how far had he come? The forests and cliffs looked nothing like the sparse steppe-forest of his home. Sick panic squeezed his heart. And the Offering!

Tarin plucked at the snow leopard skin wrapped around him. His tunic and *beaska* lay over rocks, drying in the warm sun, as well as his furs. His backpack was spread out on the beach, next to his boots and mammoth felt linings. But there was no sign of the Offering.

The breeze changed direction and Tarin caught the tantalising aroma of rich broth. With unsteady steps, he moved towards the girl. She watched him approach and tucked a strand of fair hair behind her ears. She smiled at Tarin.

'Are you hungry?'

Tarin nodded and tried to smile back. Worry creased his forehead, and he lowered himself to a rock next to her. He wanted to thank her . . . or ask where he was . . . or ask her her name . . . Any one of countless questions. Instead, he frowned.

'Why am I wearing this?' He pulled at the fur. Even to his own ears his words sounded harsh. The girl's eyes turned wary. They looked red and Tarin wondered if she had been crying.

'It was the only dry thing in your pack.' The girl leaned

over the cooking pot and stirred the broth. Tarin's stomach clenched. 'The broth is ready if you'd like some?' She handed a cup to Tarin and he clasped it in his hands. It was made from bone, and felt familiar. He recognised the shape and feel of the cup he carried from Mammoth Camp.

The girl sat back on her heels and watched him sip the liquid.

'This is good,' Tarin said, choking slightly as the hot liquid burned his throat. But he was too hungry to wait. He drained the cup and held it out for more.

'Soon.' The girl took the cup and placed it on the ground. 'Let your stomach settle first, or you'll be sick.'

Tarin nodded and rubbed his face with his hands.

'Do . . . do you mind . . . if I use your cup?' The girl sounded worried and tense. Tarin looked at her in surprise. Her eyes were on the pot of broth and she stirred it with a long, bleached bone. Her gaze flickered upwards. 'I have no cup of my own,' she said. 'I have my water flask . . . but that's about it. We had to leave in a hurry, you see.'

Tarin nodded and she filled the cup for herself. Her eyes closed as she sipped the liquid and she clasped the cup with trembling hands. Tarin wondered who she was and where she had come from. Who were her people? There was something about her words that worried him, but his brain still felt sluggish and slow. He let her words wash over him and raised his face to the sun, enjoying the warmth.

' . . . starving . . .' she was saying. 'There's less and less food to find . . .' The girl scrambled to her feet and picked her way over the rocks to the water. She splashed her face and continued talking. 'I promise I'll find something to make it up to you.' She dipped the cup into the water and handed it to Tarin.

Tarin took the cup and drank the water. It was cold and clear. Some of her words penetrated the fog around his brain.

'You were starving, too. I . . . I didn't know if you would survive . . .'

Thoughts shifted in Tarin's mind, coming together to form pictures. He stared at her in dawning realisation.

'The . . . the Offering?'

The girl frowned and shook her head. 'I don't understand. What Offering?'

Tarin stared at the pot, still half full of broth. At the fur around his shoulders. At the reindeer hide wrapped around the girl. Not part of the Offering, but still, it was the reindeer hide from his pack.

His hands clutched his hair. His stomach churned. He bent over and the cup of broth rushed up his throat and spilled on the rocky ground. Tremors clenched his stomach until it was empty.

'I told you not to eat so fast,' the girl said, jumping backwards.

Tarin shook his head. He wanted to tell her that was not the problem, but the words stuck in his throat like sharp bones.

The girl disappeared, then returned with a cup of water. Tarin took it and tried to rinse the bitter taste from his mouth, but it stayed with him.

'That food . . . the fur . . .' His voice was hoarse. 'I was to take it to the Mountain . . . but now . . .' Tarin stopped, unsure what to say. What should he tell her? That now his clan would die? Because of her, and because of him. That he would never be able to return home?

'I don't understand you.' The girl stood before him, her hands on her hips. She frowned at him with darkening eyes.

'It was the Offering!' Tarin shouted. His voice bounced off the cliff walls. He picked up a rock and hurled it into the river. 'It was an Offering to the Earth Mother.'

'Well, how was I supposed to know that!' The girl shouted back and waved her arms.

'You shouldn't have touched it!'

'You were dying –'

'Then you should have let me die –'

'Fine! Next time I will –'

'What am I going to do now?' Tarin struggled to his

174

feet and stumbled back to the cave. He felt numb. He felt helpless.

'You're still weak,' the girl's voice followed him. 'Let me help you.'

But Tarin hurried to the cave before she could reach him. He wanted to be alone. He wanted to go to sleep and never wake up. He wanted to dream of his family, but he knew their faces would bring him no comfort.

Perhaps we will see each other in death, he thought. When we walk in the Spirit World.

He heard the girl enter the cave, but he kept his eyes shut and didn't move. Her hands brushed his hair off his forehead and her fingertips felt rough against his skin. He wanted to push her away, but his limbs would no longer move. They felt as heavy as rocks.

'You have fever,' she said, her voice low and soothing. 'Drink this.'

Tarin tasted willowbark as she pressed the cup to his lips. He wanted to tell her he didn't want her medicine. Or was it his medicine? Was that, too, part of the Offering? Had he been soothed and comforted by Old Mother's herbs while lying helpless in the cave? He rolled onto his side, away from the girl.

'You should have let me drown,' he whispered, squeezing his eyes shut.

The girl didn't reply.

Tarin heard the scrape of the cup against the rocks as she placed it next to him, the scuff of her feet and her footsteps fading as she left the cave. Then there was nothing but silence. Soft, sacred silence.

Tell me about the dreams, Old Father had said.

Tarin shook his head. His dreams . . . his curse . . . how could he tell anyone? How could he say that he flew above the earth like an owl, his hearing keen and his sight sharp? They would say it was the bad Spirits . . . the bad Spirits that had been inside him from the day he was born. They would laugh at him, spit on him, and kick him into the dirt. His father would look at his son and see only shame. His mother . . . his mother would be brave, but inside, her heart would break.

But Old Father had known. He'd looked at Tarin with eyes that saw everything. Every secret. Every hidden shame.

'How did you know?'

A small owl feather was caught between two rocks. Old Father plucked it free and the wind carried it away. They watched it until it was no longer visible.

'Because I, too, have the dreams,' Old Father said. 'They are the dreams of the Spirit Keepers.'

'No!' Tarin shook his head. 'I don't want to be a Spirit Keeper.'

Old Father laughed and his eyes glowed. 'You don't want to fly like the eagles? Or run like the antelopes? You don't want to burrow deep beneath the ground like the marmots, or glide through the forests like the lynx?'

'No!' But this time Tarin's voice wavered, and Old Father heard it.

'It is not your choice, Scared Rabbit. It is the Great Mother's will. And she will ask of you a great price. One you may not be willing to pay. See ...' And Old Father pointed to the horizon. Tarin shaded his eyes and stared into the setting sun. Then he saw them.

'Mammoths!' he gasped, and then, he was there with them. He was one of them. Their pungent animal scent was all around him and he could feel the heat from their bodies. He followed along behind the herd as they pushed their way through snowfall that was growing thicker by the minute. It was heavy work. His shoulders bowed and his legs were too small and weak to push through the drifts. His thick fur was heavy with ice and snow, and he called desperately for his herd to slow down and help him. Each step became harder and more painful. He wanted to stop and rest, but he knew if he did, he would die. His fur would freeze fast to the snow, trapping him.

He cried out again, a high-pitched trumpeting. An adult female turned and called back to him, urging him on. His mother. Tarin recognised her scent, but then she, too, turned away. She had to keep up with the herd.

They were leaving him. The herd was leaving him behind!

'Mother!' Tarin cried, but he knew if she stopped, she too would perish.

He could no longer see them in a world that was completely white. But he would keep going. He would find them. One day. He lowered his head and took another step. The snow was now up to his shoulders.

Where they go, you cannot follow ...

Was that Old Father speaking to him in his dream?

'I will. I will follow them,' Tarin shouted, but then the ground he was standing on shook and trembled. It split apart, right at his feet, and he had no choice but to step back, away from the fissure that had opened before him. Steam hissed upwards, melting the snow, but the chasm was too wide to jump and the great heat from below scorched his fur.

'Mother!' he shouted, as the world trembled around him.

But they were gone. And staring down at the chasm, Tarin realised Old Father was right. He couldn't follow them. He was no longer a part of their herd.

He was alone.

A Friendship
Forms

Tarin watched the girl from the mouth of the cave. She stood by the edge of the water, hands on her hips, and stared at the cliff face opposite. Then she bent and picked up a handful of stones. She tossed them into the churning water, watching some sink and others bounce off the rocks. With each throw, she gave a little grunt of frustration. When she had cast all her rocks, she paced up and down, shoulders tensed and hands curled into fists. She kicked at the pile of bleached bones washed up on the beach and stooped to pick up the tip of an aurochs horn. She jabbed it savagely towards the rocks.

'Er . . .' Tarin cleared his throat, unsure what to say. His anger had melted away, leaving him empty inside. And his dream . . . He closed his eyes, feeling again the weight of the ice on his back and the effort to push through the snow drifts. Every detail was still with him. Every sensation. The loss. The abandonment. The desolation. He opened his eyes and dragged himself back to the real world.

The girl spun around and dropped the aurochs horn, but she, too, seemed unsure what to say. They stood on the rocky beach, studying each other.

Tarin saw a girl of about his age, but taller. Her pale hair was matted with small sticks and leaves, and her skin stretched too tightly over her narrow face. Sunken eyes stared at him warily.

'My ... my name is Tarin ... and ... you saved my life. I ... I thank you.'

Kaija let go of her breath in a gasp and words tumbled from her lips. 'You're awake! You're well! You ... you can help me.' She grabbed his wrists and the bones of her hands jutted through her skin. 'I'm sorry, so sorry, about your Offering,' the girl said. 'I didn't know.' She bit her lip and released him. 'I'll make it up to you.' Her voice was soft, almost lost in the rushing of the river.

Tarin sat down on a rock. The pallid sun warmed his face and arms. He was alive. And he still had half the Offering. He swallowed the bubble of panic that constantly threatened to choke him.

'Is ... does your clan have the sickness, too?' The sadness

in the girl's voice surprised Tarin. He looked closer, seeing lines of weariness and deep shadows beneath her eyes. Her lips were pressed together, her small fists clenching and unclenching by her side.

'No.' Tarin shook his head. 'What sickness?'

The girl shook her head and faced into the wind, letting it brush her tangled hair away from her face and eyes. Then she breathed deeply, and came and sat next to him.

'My clan has a sickness.' She kicked at the rocks beneath her feet. 'Many have died. My brother . . . he was so young.' Her voice broke, and she dropped her head, letting her hair fall over her face once more.

'I'm sorry,' Tarin said.

Kaija sniffed and tossed her head back.

'Death is a part of life, that's what they say. That's what they used to say – the Spirit Keeper and the leaders. If it's the Earth Mother's will that we walk with her in the next world. But how could it be Her will that so many die? How could it be Her will that all the children . . .' Her voice cracked and she stopped, tears welling in her eyes.

Tarin caught his breath. What sickness could destroy an entire clan? He thought of his mother and father and the rest of Mammoth Clan and felt his heart shrivel.

'How?' His voice caught in his throat. 'How could that happen? Surely your healers . . .'

Kaija almost laughed. 'My mother is the best healer in all of River Clan, but even she couldn't help.' Her voice wobbled and she dropped her head onto her knees. Tarin had to sit down on the rocks next to her to hear her as she continued. 'There's a special tea she makes using wood horsetail and dead nettle. It's difficult medicine to make, and she only uses it when someone is spitting up blood . . . and a poultice of river horsetail and sweet vernal. It eats into the wounds and weakens the evil Spirits. Then the Spirit Keeper can battle with them and drive them out with sage smoke.' Her voice faded, and she stared miserably in front of her. Tarin could tell she wasn't seeing the river rocks and running water. She was back at her camp, seeing the tormented bodies of her family and friends, smelling the heavy scented smoke mixed with the stench of festering wounds and body waste.

She shivered and rubbed her arms.

'In the end, all my mother could do was brew the mustara root tea that . . . that . . .' She stopped speaking and dropped her head again. Tarin understood. Old Mother had a special tea she brewed to relieve strong pain, and sometimes, to bring on death. She had given it to Ristak when he was gored by the bison. Tarin could still remember the bitter smell.

'She thought it was her fault, you see,' Kaija continued in

a small voice. 'She was the Healer. She should have realised how serious the sickness was. But in the beginning, it was little more than fever and stomach cramps. The weakness, the red eyes, the wounds – they all came later. And then . . .' She stopped and shivered, covering her face with her hands. 'Tarin . . . if you could hear them trying to breathe! It was as though their chests were filled with water! My mother thought the whole clan paid for her mistake, and all she could do was tell us to run. They blamed us, you see. They said we were bad luck. We didn't even have time to pack a bag, and for days we had no idea if we, too, had the illness in us.'

Tarin couldn't help but lean away. 'How do you know you don't?'

Kaija shrugged and pointed to the sun.

'That is the seventh time I have seen the sun rise since we fled our camp. And I'm still strong. But I'm not sure about Luuka.'

'Luuka?'

'My brother.' Kaija turned to Tarin and grasped him by the arms again. 'He is all I have left in the world, and now Boar Clan has him. You have to help me. Please, help me!'

Tarin prised her grip from his arms and held her hands. Her whole body was shaking. He frowned and shook his head reluctantly. He had his own quest. His clan was relying on him to save them. Again that feeling of bereavement washed over him.

'I wish I could help you,' he said slowly.

'But you won't?' Kaija pulled her hands away from him. She wiped her tears with an angry swipe.

'I can't.' Tarin's voice dropped low. 'I have to continue my own journey. I have to take whatever is left of my Offering to the Mother. I'm sorry,' he said, as Kaija turned away from him. 'I know you saved my life . . .'

'And yet you still won't help me save my brother?'

Tarin opened his mouth to speak, but he could only shake his head. He felt miserable.

'My clan is depending on me,' he said, finally. 'The Spirits told us if we don't make an Offering to the Earth Mother, Mammoth Clan will all die.'

But I am no longer a part of Mammoth Clan . . .

And there was the truth of his dream. It hit him in the chest like a spear of ice, the pain of his loss so great he nearly cried out. The herd had left him . . . and he could not follow.

'Mammoth Clan? You're Mammutti?' Kaija turned to face him, a strange glow in her eyes.

Tarin hesitated, then spoke firmly. 'Yes, I'm still Mammutti. I may be lost and I may never see them again, but I am still Mammutti, and I will keep my vow to take the Offering, what's left of it, to the Mountain and beg the Earth Mother for help and forgiveness. It is all I can do for my clan now.'

The glow in Kaija's eyes dimmed. 'My mother dreamed of mammoths one night, but I see now it had no meaning. It was simply brought on by herbs and illness.' She rubbed her face savagely. 'My clan is dead. All I have left is my brother, and I won't let him die. I'll rescue him myself!'

She stood abruptly and marched back to the cave.

'You have no supplies, no weapons,' Tarin called after her.

'I don't care,' Kaija shouted.

'No food, no spare furs –'

'I don't need them!'

'Do you at least have a plan?' Tarin's voice rang around the small canyon, bouncing off the cliffs.

Kaija stopped and looked at him. 'I have a plan,' she said, determination in her voice and the set of her jaw. 'But I need someone to help me with it.'

In the silence that followed, Tarin shook his head. Why was he hesitating? he asked himself. He had his own quest.

But if it wasn't for the girl, you would be dead, and the Offering would be lying at the bottom of the river, he reminded himself.

A bitter taste flooded his mouth and he tried to spit it out. But the voice inside his head was right – he would be dead, and his quest would have ended in failure if it weren't for Kaija.

'Tarin ...' Kaija's voice was low, and trembling. 'You are lost. Do you even know where the Great Mother's Mountain is?'

Tarin shook his head and pressed his lips together.

'If you help me save my brother,' she said, 'I'll guide you to the Mother's Mountain.'

'You'd do that?' Tarin asked, surprise in his voice.

Kaija looked at him steadily. 'I need your help, and you need mine. That's what friends are for.'

'Friends.' Tarin said the word thoughtfully, as though tasting it. He had never really considered anyone his friend before. He had Taavo and his sisters, but family was different. Friends were by choice, and no one had ever chosen him.

He looked around the canyon, the steep cliffs and foaming water, so different from the steppes. He had no knowledge of this land. No knowledge of how to find his home again, or how to continue his journey. He needed a guide, as much as Kaija needed his help now. It would be a fair trade. And maybe, if they travelled together, he wouldn't feel so alone.

'Friends,' he agreed. 'Now, what's your plan?'

Tarin fed another branch of wood to the fire and watched it catch alight. He was dressed in dry warm clothes, his belly was full of meat broth and half a salmon cake, and the pain and fever that had attacked his body for the last two days was gone. Even his bad leg wasn't aching. He stretched it out in front of him and sighed.

'I don't think your plan will work.'

Kaija glared and waved a strip of dried meat at him. 'Why not? I don't see anything wrong with it.' She tore at the meat with her teeth and munched fiercely.

Tarin ran his hand through his hair. It fell over his eyes and he wished he hadn't lost the leather thong he used to tie it back.

'There are only two of us. And how many Boar Clan?'

'At least ten men,' Kaija said. 'But we'll surprise them. They won't know we're coming.'

Tarin shook his head, thinking. 'I'm ... not strong.' It was difficult for him to say the words. He looked up, expecting to see contempt in the girl's eyes, but she waved his concerns aside.

'You don't have to be strong, just quiet and fast.'

Tarin squirmed, feeling worse. 'I can't be fast,' he said reluctantly. 'I have a weak leg. You may not have noticed.'

They sat in silence for a moment, each lost in their own thoughts.

'I didn't know,' Kaija said. 'But that doesn't matter. I'm fast. I just need you to wait by the boats.'

Tarin rubbed his nose and frowned. 'I'm not sure I can get over the cliff.'

'Of course you can,' Kaija said. 'It's narrow, but I'm sure you can do it. It just takes a bit of determination.'

A smile twitched the corners of Tarin's lips. She sounded like Saara. His breath caught painfully as he thought of his family. If it were Saara taken prisoner, you'd do anything to save her.

'I'll try,' he said. He resolved to get over that cliff even if he had to crawl the whole way. The smile he received in thanks warmed his heart.

The pine tree bridge was the first obstacle. Kaija ran lightly over the huge trunk, but Tarin wasn't so sure on his feet.

'Why don't you let me carry your backpack,' Kaija said. 'That way you'll feel more balanced. And you can use that driftwood like a walking stick.'

Tarin felt strange without the pack on his back. He remembered standing on the hilltop with his father that last morning, looking out over the steppes. The wind lashed their hair and brought with it the scent of snow in the north. His leg had ached then, despite the pain-killing tea, and the pack was heavy. He remembered staggering a little as he swung it over his shoulders. Now, it was lighter, but his heart was heavier.

The cliff path tested him, but slowly he made it to the small clearing and the pine tree. He crouched, hidden by bracken fern and low branches, and tried to breathe quietly.

'We'll stay here until dark,' Kaija murmured, keeping her voice low. 'Then you wait by the coracles. I'll get Luuka, and we'll escape down the river.'

'What about the guards?' Tarin scratched his nose and frowned.

'I'll distract them, don't worry. You just have a coracle ready to go.'

'It sounds too simple.' Tarin's breathing slowed and the thudding in his chest eased.

'The best plans are simple,' Kaija said. 'And we have the element of surprise.'

Tarin chewed his lip and nodded reluctantly. He still didn't like the plan, but he could think of no alternative. He followed Kaija further into the forest cover and they sat in silence, waiting for darkness to fall.

Hours later, the light had finally faded, and it was safe to move from their hiding place. Kaija watched Tarin as the growing darkness swallowed him. She could see the weakness in his leg when he walked, but to her, his limp was minor. She knew a man from down river who was unable to walk without a stick. Her mother had treated him after a woolly rhinoceros crushed his legs and gouged him so severely it was doubtful he would live. But her mother had treated him and bullied him to walk again, despite his pain making the cave walls echo with his screams.

Her mother was ruthless like that, but a good healer often had to be harsh. Kaija had always thought she couldn't do it . . . she couldn't be as cold as her mother, but now – she shivered again – she realised she was more like her mother than she had thought. Hadn't she forced Tarin into helping her?

'I will do anything to save you, Luuka,' she whispered beneath her breath. She felt a qualm as Tarin disappeared from view. She hoped he would understand. She wondered about the Mammutti boy – about where he came from and who his people were. She could see his injury wasn't new, and she wondered how it had happened.

When she could no longer see him, she moved forward. The only light was from the large cooking fire outside the main hut, and she strained her ears for sounds that would warn her of danger. Muffled voices came from one of the huts. A baby cried, then quietened. A flap of hide covering the doorway blew open. In the gloom, it looked like a wounded animal, twisting in pain.

Kaija breathed slowly to still the pounding of her heart, and crept quietly past.

She hid in the shadows of the hut closest to Luuka's prison. How desperately she wanted to see him, to speak to him, but she had other things to do first. She hurried to where the overhanging branches of the forest shaded a deep pile of fallen leaves and gathered them into a pile. Then she drew from her belt the aurochs horn she had found on the beach. Inside it, nestled in dried fungus and ash, was a coal from their fire. She leaned close and gently breathed on it until it glowed red.

She lowered the coal to the tinder and blew harder. Slowly the flames took hold. The scent of wood smoke tickled her nose, and she quickly glanced around. She didn't want her fire to be discovered too fast. She fed some larger branches to the flames and watched it grow.

Somewhere, an argument broke out. Kaija heard angry voices, male and female. The flap to a hut burst open and a young man strode forward. He stopped, surprised by the glow of the fire and the strange girl crouching next to it.

Kaija had no choice. She had to raise the alarm now, startle the camp into action before her plan failed. She lifted her head and screamed: 'Fire!'

The flames roared high and the sharp, bitter tang of wood smoke filled the air. Kaija pressed herself against Luuka's hut as men and women rushed past with pots of water and heavy hides.

'Luuka!' she whispered urgently through the wooden branches of his prison.

There was no answer and she called again, banging against the twisted branches and struggling to undo the thick leather thong that held his door closed.

'Kaija?' Luuka pushed his hands through the gaps in the branches to reach for her. 'What are you doing here? You'll be caught!'

'Help me, Luuka. I can't untie the knots.' She cast a swift look over her shoulder. 'Hurry.'

'Kaija, just get away from here! Run!'

'No!' She kicked hard at the door and heard it crack. She threw her whole body against the door, and it splintered beneath her. She fell forward in a heap of tangled branches and scratched arms and legs.

'Come on!' She grabbed Luuka's wrist and pulled him out of the hut.

The camp was in chaos as they ran. The fire was under control, but the air was still thick with smoke. It burned Kaija's lungs and stung her eyes. She glanced at Luuka, who was hobbling beside her and clutching his ribs where the

Boar Clan hunters had kicked him.

Kaija kept her hand clasped around his wrist as she pulled him towards the river.

'Kaija, wait . . .' Luuka fell to his knees, drawing in large gasps of air. His face twisted in pain as he spoke. 'I think my ribs might be broken.'

Kaija looked down at him in dismay. 'Just a little further. Come on, Luuka. You can do it.'

Luuka shook his head. He was having trouble breathing. Sweat dripped from his brow and his hair fell over his eyes in lank strands. Mud and dried blood caked his clothes.

'You go.' He tried to push her away. A shout from behind told them they had been seen. 'Run, Kaija! While you can.'

But Kaija stayed where she was. 'No. I'm not leaving you.'

'I'm the elder, and I say to go.' Luuka's voice was an angry growl. 'Now!'

He pushed her with all his strength and groaned, but before she could turn and run, two Boar Clan hunters rushed them, spears raised. One of them clamped his arms around Kaija, and the other raised his spear like a club and hit Luuka over the side of the head. He fell to one knee, blood gushing from his temple.

'No!' Kaija screamed, kicking and fighting her captor. But the arms around her were strong and didn't let go.

Another hunter ran at them – a tall girl with many

decorative beads covering her tunic.

'Another dirty little thief.' She spat on the ground and peered closely at Kaija. 'And from the same litter as this one.' She kicked Luuka and he gasped for breath.

Kaija screamed and lashed out towards the girl with a savage kick that caught her in the stomach.

The girl's breath rushed from her lungs and she doubled over in pain. She glared at Kaija with furious eyes, and whipped a thin flint blade from her belt.

'Dirty hyena,' she growled.

Luuka grunted and swung his fists blindly to protect his sister.

The girl just laughed and pushed him back into the mud. 'I will deal with you next.'

She turned again to Kaija, but as she did, Tarin exploded from the shadows with a mighty yell, brandishing a flaming torch in his hands. His eyes were wild and his lips drawn back in a snarl. He waved his torch towards the hunters.

Kaija's captor took a step back from the flame, releasing his grip. It was enough for Kaija to twist and bite down hard on his ungloved hand. With a scream of pain, her captor released her.

'Kaija!' Luuka shouted. 'Run! Now!'

There was no way to win. More hunters were running towards them, waving spears, and Tarin's torch was slowly dying. Light snowflakes dampened the last of the flames.

'Tarin,' Kaija cried. 'Run!' And she turned and ran for the cover of the forest.

Prisoners

'Tarin! Run!'

Tarin heard the words, but he didn't want to run. He felt strong. His blood sizzled in his veins. His heart was on fire. He saw the way the Boar Clan hunter dug his fingers into Kaija's arms and he wanted to attack him. The hunter was twice her height, and broad-shouldered. He could snap Kaija's neck with his bare hands.

For a moment, Tarin imagined it was Miika standing there in front of him, and he wanted to smash his flaming branch into his teeth. It was a strong branch of oak, and the hunters watched him carefully as he waved the flame in front of them. Kaija is not a hyena, a dirty scavenger of carrion, he thought angrily. These people are the animals, torturing the frightened and the weak.

The boy lying on the ground was covered in blood. He groaned, and Tarin realised he was still alive. He tried to

196

move forward, but the girl with the knife snarled at him. Her cold eyes reminded Tarin of a savage animal. Another hunter feinted in his direction, rushing forward, then back. Tarin waved his branch and the hunter retreated.

'Farla, end this!'

The girl with the knife – Farla – turned her snarl on the speaker, and Tarin's eyes followed her.

It was a mistake. He didn't see the hunter with the heavy oak staff until it was too late. He caught a blur of movement out of the corner of his eye, and turned, just as the staff connected with the side of his face. It was lucky he turned. The staff, wielded with such strength, would have crushed his skull. Lights exploded. The impact rippled through his body. Blackness swooped on Tarin like a flock of ravens, robbing his eyes of sight. But he could still hear.

'Durk! He was mine.' The rage in the girl's voice was palpable.

'You were too slow, Farla. Learn from this.'

Tarin heard scuffling, then he was lifted by his arms and dragged along the rocky ground.

'Take them to the drop hole. Tomorrow, at Sundown, they will journey to meet the Spirits.'

'They should have met the Spirits tonight,' Farla snarled, and a heavy boot slammed into Tarin's stomach.

Tarin tasted blood and bitter bile as it rushed up his

throat. He could no longer hear over the rushing noise in his head. Like a great wave, it grabbed him and pulled him under. And then there was nothing.

Tears blinded Kaija and her hair tangled in branches as she stumbled blindly through the forest. The light mist had thickened and now snowflakes fell, making the uneven ground slick. She couldn't see in the darkness and fell often, scraping hands and knees.

She dared not stop. Behind, she could hear sounds of thudding feet and shouting. The light from flaming torches flickered through the trees. Boar Clan were searching for her. Again.

She heard a cry of pain, and she spun around. 'Tarin!' She hesitated, unsure what to do.

I should go back. I have to help them. But what if I'm caught, too? She shook her head, confused. *But I can't just leave them! This is all my fault!*

Kaija turned to run back to the camp, but a low root caught her foot and she fell, hitting her head against a rock. She felt sticky warm blood trickle down the side of her face. A great wail rose inside her.

Everything had gone wrong.

She sat on the forest floor, in the damp leaves and mud,

and let the snow fall around her. She pushed her palms into her eyes and struggled for breath through the tight band of fear that wound around her chest, crushing her.

'Over here! I hear something.'

Kaija clapped her hands over her mouth to stop any sound escaping. A light was weaving through the trees, closer now. Branches crashed. Voices grew louder.

Frantically, Kaija edged back into the tangle of bushes behind her. A hazelnut bush scratched her face and arms, but she wriggled further into the concealing branches and pulled them close around her.

If it were daylight, they would have found her for sure. Even a child would have been able to track her through the soft ground and disturbed undergrowth, but the night gave her sanctuary and the falling snowflakes blurred her tracks.

'You're hearing things, Farla,' a man's voice said. He raised the burning torch in his hand and flickering light swept the area.

Farla hissed in anger and jabbed at the undergrowth with her spear. Kaija held her breath as the girl came closer, and shrank further back into the bushes.

'I know I heard something.' Farla stopped by the hazelnut bush. Kaija could see the beads on her tunic gleam white through the branches.

'Broda has found something,' said the man.

'No, I haven't,' another girl replied quickly. Through the branches, Kajia glimpsed a short, stocky girl bend to the ground, then jump quickly to hide her hands behind her back. It was the girl who had been cooking down by the river. Kaija recognised the hunched shoulders and broad, flat face. She stared sulkily at Farla.

'What have you got, Broda?' Farla towered over the cringing girl.

Broda took a step back. 'N . . . nothing.' Her eyes scanned the forest, searching for escape.

'You have something behind your back.' Farla moved closer again, so close they were almost touching, and smiled coldly at Broda. Kaija shivered.

'I . . . I haven't.' Broda glanced uneasily at the man. He leant back against a tree and folded his arms. 'I haven't.' She squeaked as Farla grabbed her by the arm. 'You're hurting me,' she cried.

Farla twisted Broda's arm and forced her fist open, taking something from it.

The man pushed off the tree and sauntered over to the girls. He looked at the object now resting in Farla's palm. 'It's a bead,' he said.

'My bead.' Farla glared at Broda. 'You stole this from me.'

'I . . . I didn't.' Broda took a step away from Farla and wet her lips. 'It was there, on the ground. I found it –'

'You stole it!' Farla pushed Broda in the chest and she stumbled backwards.

'I was going to return it. It must have fallen off your tunic.'

Farla looked down at her top. Where Kaija had kicked her, a row of beads had come loose. Farla screamed in anger.

'Look what that thief has done! I will make her pay!'

She swung her spear in fury. Broda squealed and tried to move back, but her foot caught a rock and she fell. Kaija bit back a cry as Farla's spear just missed the fallen girl.

'Enough of this.' The man stepped forward and grasped Farla's spear. She glared at him, and for a moment they stood, chest to chest.

Then Farla snorted and wrenched her spear from the man's grasp. 'You surprise me, Durk, protecting these thieves. I had thought you stronger than that.' She snorted again and stalked away from them.

Broda climbed shakily to her feet, then she and Durk followed, their boots crunching on the newly fallen snow.

Kaija waited until she could no longer hear them moving through the forest. With their torch gone, it was dark once more, and the snow cover was thicker. But the hazelnut bush protected her from the worst of the snowfall.

Now the immediate danger had passed, her body started shaking. She carefully slid Tarin's pack off her back and found his furs. She wrapped them around herself and slowly her shivering subsided.

She wondered where Luuka and Tarin were, sure that neither had escaped. The image of her brother's bloody face flashed through her mind. And what of Tarin? He had been reluctant to help her, and now he, too, was a prisoner. She placed her hands over her ears and tried to drown out the sound of his cry.

She started shivering again, this time from fear. What was she going to do now? The thought filled her mind. She didn't know when her hands left her ears and crept to the pendant at her throat.

Spirit of Horse, help me.

Her fingers traced the shape carved into the bone. Four vertical lines, for the four strong legs of the horse, galloping over the plains. She wished she were a horse and could just run and run forever with no end. She wanted to feel the wind in her mane, and the thud of her hooves striking the ground. She wanted to run away, and never come back.

But I can't leave Luuka and Tarin here.

Kaija's head sank onto her knees. A great weariness washed over her, and she huddled further into the furs.

'Help me, Spirit of Horse,' she whispered beneath her breath. 'Help me to be strong.' And help me to not run away and leave Luuka and Tarin behind.

The sound of crashing branches and a shower of cold, wet snow woke Kaija in the moorning.

'I know you're in there,' said a voice, rattling the branches so more snow fell through. 'You'd better come out now.'

Kaija crawled from her hiding place and rubbed her eyes. Judging by the pale light filtering through the trees, it was still early. Her breath misted the air around her, and she looked in surprise at Broda.

'I heard you last night.' Broda pointed a short, sharp spear towards Kaija's throat.

Kaija swallowed. 'Why didn't you catch me then?'

A sly smile spread over Broda's face. 'Because then Farla would take the credit. Now you're my catch.'

Kaija shivered, but it wasn't from the cold. Plans rushed through her mind, but she discarded each one. Broda looked slow and clumsy, but the point of her spear was tipped with flint, and she hefted it comfortably in her hands. It looked like the spear that had thudded into the tree. Kaija wondered again how anyone could throw a spear with such force. Maybe because they were shorter spears than the ones River Clan used, but it would still take a lot of strength to force a spear through a tree. Maybe Boar Clan had a magic known only to them. Kaija felt the small hairs on the back of her neck prickle. She couldn't fight magic.

Broda was searching the ground. She kicked up leaves

with her feet and used the spear to turn over small rocks. When she realised what she was looking for, an idea suddenly came to Kaija.

'That bead you found last night was beautiful,' she said, careful to keep her voice calm.

Broda stopped her search and frowned. She lifted her spear and pointed it at Kaija. 'You shouldn't be talking.'

Kaija nodded and slipped the fox fur from her shoulder. 'Can I put my fur away in my pack? Is that all right?'

Broda looked at her suspiciously, but nodded.

'It was Farla's bead, wasn't it?' Kaija continued, taking her time to roll the fur. She kept her eyes down, but she was aware of Broda shifting her weight from one foot to the other. 'She had so many. Do you have any beads?' Kaija risked a small glance up.

'No.' Broda shook her head. Thick brown plaits swung either side of her face. Kaija stayed silent, pretending she was having trouble with the knots on the pack. Soon, Broda continued. 'Farla is Borik's daughter. She has the beads, because she ... she's more important.'

'I could see that.' Kaija unlaced the leather thongs. 'She must be the most important girl in the clan.'

'No, she's not!' Broda's voice was sharp. Her mouth turned down at the corners and she glared at Kaija. 'I liked it better when Ern One-Arm was our leader.'

'And Borik is your leader now?'

Broda nodded and jabbed the tip of the spear into the ground. 'Since last Fall. They say Ern was sick, but everyone knows Borik dropped him down the Spirit Hole.'

'The what?'

'The Spirit Hole. It's in the big cave behind the camp. Borik says it leads to the Spirit World. And tonight we're having a special ceremony. There'll be lots of food, and Durk and the hunters have caught a couple of wolves to sacrifice. And you and your friends will be dropped down the Spirit Hole.'

'What!' Shock made Kaija's voice squeak and Broda jumped back and raised the spear again. Kaija swallowed hard and clasped her hands to stop them shaking. 'Then they are still alive?'

'Of course.' A smile spread across Broda's face, but her eyes glittered hungrily. 'That way the Spirits will be more grateful. They will give us power over our enemies.'

Kaija bent forward over the pack so Broda wouldn't see her close her eyes briefly. She took a deep breath and opened the pack. 'And of course Farla will be there wearing that beautiful tunic with all the beads.' She glanced up in time to see the frown descend on Broda's face once more.

'Everyone will be there,' Broda said.

Kaija pushed the fox furs into the pack and slid her hand

down towards the small parcel at the bottom. Her fingers closed over the two carved beads. 'And you don't have any beads?'

Broda shook her head.

'Would you like a bead?' Kaija drew her hand out of the pack, but kept it closed.

Broda looked at her sharply. 'You are playing a trick on me?'

'No trick,' said Kaija. 'A simple trade. You let me go, and I'll give you one of my beads.' And she opened her hand.

Broda drew her breath in sharply at the sight of the two creamy beads nestled in Kaija's palm. She reached out to them, but Kaija closed her fist and drew them away.

'Trade first,' she said.

Broda nodded and licked her lips. Then her eyes narrowed. 'I could just take those beads off you when I take you back to camp.'

'Maybe.' Kaija nodded. 'But then I'd tell everyone you had them, and Farla would take them off you. She would have more beads . . . and you would have none.'

The frown on Broda's face deepened. 'And what if I let you go?'

'Then I give you a bead. For your very own.'

Broda studied her, then raised the spear menacingly. 'Two beads.'

Kaija bit her lips to stop them stretching into a smile. She forced herself to speak slowly, and reluctantly shook her head. 'These are precious beads, carved by my mother's mother, who was a great Spirit Keeper.'

Broda's eyes opened wide and she breathed out, the chill air swirling white around her. 'Are they sacred beads?'

'Very sacred.' Kaija nodded solemnly. 'They give great protection to whoever has them. If I were to give you both ...'

'Yes?' Broda asked eagerly as Kaija paused and glanced around.

'If I were to give you both,' Kaija opened her hand again and turned the beads to show the fine carvings on the smooth surface, 'I would have to ask more in return.'

'What do you want?' Broda leaned close.

Kaija could smell fish on her breath, but she didn't move away. Instead, she leaned even closer.

'I want you to show me the Spirit Hole.'

A Strange Alliance

Wet earth pressing down on him. Darkness with no end.

Tarin woke with a start, clawing at the ground. He was lying on rocks, in a cave ... but ... he squinted upwards, to where pale light filtered through overhanging vines and a gaping hole in the roof. Not the cave of his nightmares.

The panic in his chest eased, and he looked around. Rocky floor, jumbled boulders, the sound of birds as they dived through the broken roof and circled the cave. Starlings, Tarin thought. He followed the flight of one as it swooped low, then speared upwards into the air once more. Tarin tried to move, but a rope of woven fur bound him securely to a wooden stake driven deep into the ground. His head hurt, his leg hurt, and his mouth tasted of dust and blood.

He struggled to sit up. As he did, he heard a low,

menacing growl. The hairs on the back of his neck rose and he froze, staring at two glowing eyes.

'She won't hurt you,' said a voice. 'She's tied up, too.'

Tarin looked closer and saw the eyes belonged to a silver-grey she-wolf. A rope was wrapped around her neck, cutting her flesh. She growled again, softer this time, and lay her head down on her paws with a whimpering sigh. Tarin frowned at the dark band of fur around her leg. An elusive memory flickered through his mind, but it disappeared like mist.

Two small bundles of dark grey fur stirred by the she-wolf's side. One opened its eyes and studied Tarin curiously, then yawned and went back to sleep. The other stood on wobbling legs and released a stream of urine. It whimpered and sniffed the mess it had made, before sneezing in disgust.

Tarin had never been so close to a living wolf, and he watched them in open-mouthed wonder and fear.

'I'm Luuka,' said the boy.

Tarin turned from the wolves to study Kaija's brother. One side of his face was heavily bruised and a gash on his head was crusted with dried blood. His cheeks were hollow, and his tunic covered in mud. He had Kaija's fair hair and the same blue eyes, but Kaija's fierceness was missing.

Tarin shifted uncomfortably on the rocks. His gaze flew back to the wolves, but they didn't move. 'I'm Tarin.'

Luuka nodded. 'You were with my sister.'

Memory returned in a rush. 'Kaija?' Tarin said urgently, looking around the cave. The wolf's eyes followed his movements. 'Did she escape?'

'I think so.' Luuka winced in pain as he shifted position. His lips thinned and he frowned at Tarin. 'She should never have tried to rescue me. Why did you let her?'

'Me? Let her?' Tarin said. 'She said if I didn't help her she'd do it herself. And she would have.'

Luuka's face relaxed and he shrugged. His moment of spirited anger had obviously tired him. 'That sounds like my sister.' He sighed and closed his eyes. 'Tonight, this will all be over,' he murmured. 'Kaija should be long gone by now.'

Tarin shook his head. 'No.' He pulled at the ropes to test their strength. 'I bet you anything you like that Kaija is hiding somewhere close by, planning some way to rescue us.'

A reluctant smile broke out on Luuka's face. 'I think you're right. How long have you known my sister?'

Tarin thought back. 'Three days,' he said in surprise. It seemed a lot longer. 'She saved my life.'

'She has a habit of doing that,' said Luuka. 'But not this time.'

A low growl from the wolf drew their attention. Her lips were pulled back and her fur was raised. She stared at the mouth of the cave. An old Boar Clan woman hobbled towards them, holding a large wooden staff decorated with feathers and bone. She raised the staff in the air and shook it at them. Her voice rose in a singsong chant, but Tarin didn't understand her words.

'Their Spirit Keeper.' Luuka's mouth was a grim line.

She came closer, and again shook the staff. Now Tarin could see her face was smeared with ash and black ochre. Her long hair was caked with mud and hung around her in woolly lengths. A bone passed through one side of her nose and out the other.

'Oi oi oi aaaaah,' she wailed, rolling her eyes back in her head until only the whites showed.

'She thinks to scare us,' said Luuka.

'She is,' said Tarin.

The wailing grew louder, and the woman shook the staff fiercely. Bones threaded through lengths of leather clanked against the wood. Animal bones or human bones? wondered Tarin with a shiver.

The Spirit Keeper brought her face close to him, and her overpowering scent of old sweat and rotten meat made his stomach turn. Green pus oozed from the bone in her nose. She gripped his chin and he struggled to get away, but she was strong for such an old woman. She spat full on his face, then used her hand to spread the saliva around. It stank of mould.

The wolf snarled and snapped in fury. She pulled against her restraint, driving the leather thong deeper into her wounded neck. The Spirit Keeper laughed and rattled her staff. She took a pouch from around her neck and shook out a handful of powder. Then she darted forward and tossed the powder in the animal's face. The wolf yelped and retreated. The woman laughed.

'Wormwood and horseradish powder,' Luuka said, his eyes blazing. He strained against his own restraint. 'She causes pain to trapped animals, to show how strong she is. But it is all an illusion. She is weak! Weak!'

Tarin wondered that Luuka could speak so bravely, but the old woman laughed at him and tossed the two boys a strip of meat.

'Eat, little worms. You must have food in your bellies for your big journey to the Spirit World. Then they will see how well we care for you.' She turned from them and hobbled towards an inky cavity at the back of the cave where she started her chant again, first waving her arms above her head, and then dipping them into another hanging pouch and slapping red-stained handprints on the rocks.

'That's the Spirit Hole.' Luuka's voice was flat. 'Where they throw their dead. And some that aren't dead.'

Tarin shuddered. He imagined an unearthly coldness seeping from the dark hole, reaching for him. He wrenched his gaze away. He looked at the strip of meat in his hand and his nose wrinkled. 'Wolverine.'

'And probably very old,' said Luuka. The wolf whimpered and edged towards him, dragging her stomach along the ground. Luuka smiled at her and tossed her his strip of meat. She sniffed it suspiciously, then snapped it up. She watched Luuka with steady eyes. When she had finished, she dropped her head onto her paws and turned her gaze on Tarin. He squirmed uneasily, noticing the patches of raw skin and the way her bones showed through her fur.

'Why the wolves?' Tarin asked. 'And why us.'

Luuka shrugged. 'I think it's their way of showing their power over their enemies. But it isn't true power.'

Tarin sniffed the meat once more and wondered what Luuka thought true power was. Hunger? Pain? The Boar Clan's Spirit Keeper had the power to inflict both those, and more besides. Fear . . . that was her power. So maybe if he wasn't frightened, she would have no power over him. Her chant rose again, echoing around the cavern. Tarin jumped as a bird swooped low, nearly grazing his head. I am protected by Owl. He held onto that thought and repeated it to himself. He hoped it would give him courage when he faced the Spirit Hole.

'If you don't want your meat, give it to her. She won't harm you,' Luuka said.

Tarin looked at the she-wolf sitting patiently before him. 'That's what you say.' Her teeth looked very sharp, he thought.

'That's what she's telling you,' said Luuka. 'See how quietly she sits, waiting.'

Tarin took the strip of meat and tossed it. Quickly the wolf pounced and swallowed it. Her pups, smelling food, whined and crawled over her, licking her muzzle with their little tongues.

'Watch this,' Luuka whispered, his eyes never leaving the wolves.

The she-wolf stood and shook off her pups. They bounded around her, snapping and snarling, as she retched and brought up a watery mess of chewed meat. The pups fell on the food and gulped it down.

'That's how she feeds them,' Luuka said, and his voice sounded as though he were fighting back tears. 'She is starving herself . . . she has no more milk. She gives everything to them, to make sure her babies survive.'

The pups sniffed the floor of the cave, then when they could find no more food, they curled into little balls and snuggled into their mother's warmth. The she-wolf licked their fuzzy heads and curled herself around them.

Tarin shook his head in amazement. 'But . . . but they are animals,' he said.

'And Boar Clan are human beings.' Luuka's gaze returned to the Spirit Keeper. She had finished her chanting and was coming back towards them.

'Now you must bathe,' she said. 'Purify yourself for the Spirits.' She waved her arms and a shadow waiting by the cave entrance scurried towards her.

'Go and bring your father.' She cuffed the young boy around the head. He hurried away, returning shortly with a tall, fierce-looking hunter. 'It is time these two were made ready,' she said. 'Take them to the river.'

'You interrupt my spear training for this?' The hunter frowned at her.

'Do not presume to question me, Durk.' The Spirit Keeper hit him with the staff. 'Your games mean nothing to me.'

Durk scowled, but said nothing more. He hauled the two boys to their feet and wrapped the leather thong around their necks. 'Try anything and I will break your necks. I do not care whether you enter the Spirit Hole alive or dead,' he hissed.

The boys stumbled after him, blinking in the brighter light of day as they moved out of the cave. Tarin realised they were now at the southern end of the camp, halfway up a hill. From where he was, he looked down on the river and the huts and across to the cliff path that led back to the pine tree bridge and rocky beach.

'Move!' Durk pushed Tarin and he lurched forward. Loose rocks slipped under his feet and he stumbled unsteadily down the hill to the flat by the river. A group of men and boys sitting around the cooking fire laughed and jeered at them. Half-finished spears lay scattered on the ground. An elderly man, his face puckered with scars, lashed a bone tip to the end of one, and another man stuffed grass into a leather pad to use as a target.

'Durk! When you have finished playing mother to those two, come and test the strength of your arm.'

Durk waved but didn't stop. One of the small boys sitting around the fire threw a bone at them. It struck Luuka on the shoulder, and the men roared with laughter. A girl carrying a large bladder of water stopped what she was doing and stared open-mouthed at them.

'Get about your work,' Durk snarled, and forced the boys to keep moving to the river.

They waded out knee-deep and, holding him by the back of his neck, Durk forced Tarin under the water until he thought his lungs would burst. He tried to scratch the hands that held him so strongly, but the man just laughed. Finally, he released Tarin and pulled him up.

Tarin gasped and coughed. Water streamed from his hair and sodden fur, and he lay shivering on the riverbank while

Luuka suffered the same treatment. Durk left them there on the bank while he joined the men around the fire. The weak sun did little to warm them.

'Tarin,' Luuka whispered. 'See over there, that man with the spear?'

Tarin followed Luuka's gaze. At the other end of the camp, the leather target had been set against a tree. The man with the scarred face paced out the distance.

'He'll never make that,' Tarin said. 'That's too far!'

'But look at their spears.' Luuka kept his voice low. He cupped his hands and blew on them.

'They're short,' said Tarin. He raised an eyebrow towards Luuka. 'You know something about these spears. What is it?'

Luuka shook his head. 'You'll see.'

Tarin frowned. He was cold and hungry, and he didn't want to play guessing games. 'They're thinner than the spears my clan use to hunt with. Such a thin spear would never bring down a mammoth or a bison.' He watched the man pick up a short, flat stick with a leather strap wrapped around it to form a loop. 'And what's that? That's not a spear. That wouldn't hit anything.'

'Quiet and watch,' said Luuka.

Tarin bit his lip, but didn't answer. The scarred man laid his spear along the stick and then, holding onto the leather loop, cast towards the target. The back of the stick rose in the air and pushed the spear further than the arm of a hunter ever could. It landed with a thud in the leather pad.

'Hah!' the man shouted. 'Match that, Durk.'

Durk nodded his head. 'A respectable throw, for an old man. But let me show you how it's done.'

He chose his own spear from the pile. This one was tipped with flint and the shaft of the spear notched with two feathers. Again, the flat stick rose to push the spear higher and faster. This time, the spear not only landed in the target – it split it in two and drove into the tree behind it.

Tarin swallowed hard. He couldn't take his eyes off the spear where it hung stuck in the tree trunk.

'How?' he whispered.

'It's the spear thrower,' Luuka said. 'I saw them using them the first day I was captured. Some say the Spirits sent Borik a vision of the spear thrower, and that's how he became leader.'

'I've never known Spirits to work like that,' Tarin murmured. His thoughts were full of the spear thrower. With a weapon like that, even he could hunt. If he could adapt the design to fit the heftier spears of the Mammutti ... and with a larger tip ... something more like the long, sharp flint blades Jarrko made, that would pass through the thick hides of the mammoth ...

'Others say he stole the idea off the last leader, Ern One-Arm, and then killed him.'

'That sounds right,' said Tarin. Then he sighed. What was he thinking? Adapt the spear thrower? He would never get the chance. This evening, at Last Light, he and Luuka were to be thrown into the Spirit Hole. They would never get the chance to try the spear throwers for themselves, and they would never get the chance to hunt with them.

'Move, worms.' Durk shoved them to their feet and pushed them back towards the cave. He lashed them once more to the stake, tightening their bonds until the ties cut into their flesh.

'Won't be long now.' He laughed as he turned to leave. 'The light fades fast this time of year.'

Tarin dropped his head onto his knees. His clothes were wet and the chill air in the cave made him shiver. He looked over towards the she-wolf. She lay with her head on her paws, watching him, then she lifted her head and howled – a haunting sound, calling to her lost pack. Tarin felt an echo of her pain deep inside and he mourned for his own lost family. Was it here his journey was going to end?

'What's your totem?' he asked Luuka.

'Horse,' said Luuka. They were sitting back to back, and no longer able to see each other. Tarin thought his voice sounded strained. 'What's yours?'

'Owl,' said Tarin. 'I am Tarin of Mammoth Clan, pro-tected by Owl.'

'Hmm . . . Mammoth Clan. Isn't that a northern clan?'

'One of the Mammutti clans,' Tarin said.

'I am Luuka, son of Senja, healer of the Third Cave of the River Clan. Protected by Horse. It is nice to meet you, Tarin of the Mammoths. It is a shame we meet only now, when we are about to meet the Spirits.'

The Spirit
Hole

Kaija stood staring at the small opening in the hillside. It was no bigger than an animal burrow.

'That's your secret way to the Spirit Hole?' She rubbed sweaty palms down her leggings and chewed her lip. 'Isn't there any other way?'

'Unless you want to march through the camp, this is the only way.' Broda stood back with her hands on her hips. 'Now give me my bead.'

'Not yet.' Kaija squinted into the hole, but the blackness inside was absolute. Cold, stale air touched her face, hinting at a passage of great depth. 'And this leads to the Spirit Hole?'

'It leads to the main cave. The Spirit Hole is there.'

'And Luuka and Tarin are in the main cave?'

'Until Last Light, then they'll be thrown into the Spirit Hole. No one comes back from the Spirit Hole.'

Kaija shivered and swallowed hard. The small passage-way could be a trap, but she had no choice. She would have to trust Broda. Then a thought occurred to her.

'How did you know about this tunnel?'

She glanced up in time to see a sulky look cloud the girl's face again.

Broda shrugged. 'I was ... checking ... the Offerings one day, on the ledge near the Spirit Hole. Sometimes, to ask the Spirits for special favours, people leave offerings of food or weapons or ...'

'Beads?'

Broda glared at Kaija and thrust her jaw forward. 'Or beads.'

'And you were caught?' Kaija imagined the scene. Broda sneaking into the cave and then hearing approaching foot-steps. The only place to hide – a small cavity in the rocks.

'This tunnel leads down to a cave off the main chamber.'

'And no one else knows about it?' Kaija didn't want to be walking into a trap or a dead end. She frowned suspiciously as Broda hesitated. 'Well? Does anyone else know about this secret tunnel?'

Broda scratched her nose and sniffed. 'I think Hela, the Spirit Keeper, does. Sometimes, when she's doing a ceremony, she just appears out of nowhere. Everyone else thinks it's because she's magic, but I watch her. I think she uses the tunnel.'

Kaija nodded her head. The River Clan shaman often did the same. They used tricks and misdirection – powdered herbs to create mist, fermented drinks that affected the mind, darkened caves and flickering shadows. She imagined a secret tunnel would be very useful.

Broda shuffled her feet impatiently. 'You must hurry.'

Kaija glanced at the pale sun overhead. The day was half gone. By Last Light, she and the boys had to be a long way from Boar Camp.

'Give me my bead now,' said Broda.

'No.' Kaija shook her head. 'This could still be a trap, or it may not lead to the cave.'

'But I told you it does!' Broda clenched her fists and stepped towards Kaija.

Kaija didn't flinch. 'When I've found the cave, then you can have the bead.'

'But what if you're caught? Then I don't get my bead! And I'm not going down there with you. If they catch me, I'll be thrown in the Spirit Hole, too.'

Kaija chewed her lip, thinking. 'Then wait by the main entrance. Try and look like you're busy, then if someone comes, you can warn me.'

'How?'

'I don't know.' Kaija dropped to her hands and knees. 'Hoot like an owl or throw some rocks or something.' Then she took a deep breath, and crawled into the darkness.

The tunnel was larger than she first thought, and Kaija was able to walk with her shoulders hunched. It was black, but a faint light from above penetrated a short way, showing her grey rock walls, a low ceiling and a twisting downward slope. But the slope was steep, and more than once Kaija felt herself slipping. She kept both hands stretched in front of her, and felt her way down. The ceiling dipped lower, forcing her to crawl once more on hands and knees. The pack on her back scraped the rock roof.

It was dark now, the twisting tunnel shutting off any light from above or below, and the air felt different, as though she were in a much larger cave. Kaija reached forward with one hand, but encountered only empty space where the ground should be. Her heart plummeted and she froze, scared to move forward, scared to move backwards. Rushing noise filled her head.

Broda! she hissed under her breath. The sound echoed in the rocky cavity. Panic threatened to overwhelm her.

Think, Kaija. Think.

She unclenched her fists and took a long, slow breath. Maybe there was a turning she missed? But as she crouched in the darkness, she realised two things: a cold breeze was blowing upward from the shaft in front of her, and sounds drifted from below, magnified and distorted. Voices, and . . . Kaija gasped as an unearthly howl filled the darkness. Was that the Spirits? Her blood pounded through her veins. Her heart raced, and small, shivery bumps covered her body.

Spirit of Horse, help!

Her breath caught in her throat in painful little gasps. She turned, ready to fly back through the tunnel, and cracked her head on the low rock.

This is what you wanted, she told herself severely. You wanted to reach the Spirit Hole.

But I didn't want any Spirits to be there!

To go back was unthinkable. She would have to give up all thoughts of rescuing Luuka and Tarin. To go forward was impossible. Broda said no one ever came back from the Spirit Hole. Kaija rocked back and forth on her heels, undecided. If Broda was telling the truth and the tunnel led to the main cave, there must be a way down the shaft.

Her hand reached forward, to the edge of the rock. Then she swung her legs around and sat on the edge. There was definitely a breeze blowing from below, so it wasn't a dead end. Kaija swallowed and her mouth felt dry. Before she could change her mind, she turned over onto her stomach.

She balanced against the edge of the shaft, and then stretched her legs downwards. Her feet scrabbled against the vertical walls. Her arms burned and her fingers ached, clutching onto the rock, but then her feet found a small ledge. She eased her weight onto it and drew in a large, shuddering breath.

She found another handhold, and reached one leg down. This time, she felt a solid rock beneath, and stepped down onto it. Another large rocky step, and another, and soon, Kaija was at the bottom of the shaft. She sat down on the sandy floor until her arms and legs had stopped shaking.

Now the murmur of voices was clearer. She followed the sound and the touch of the breeze to a small tunnel that ran off the main shaft. A faint light shone, and Kaija moved quietly now, certain she was almost at the main cavern.

The light grew stronger. Now she could see the tunnel walls, the rocks, her own hands in front of her face. She hurried along the passage as fast as she dared. A voice spoke, and Kaija's heart leapt. The words were muffled and indistinct, but there was something familiar in the tone and rhythm.

'Luuka!' She breathed the word.

The tunnel opened out suddenly, but its entrance was hidden from the main cavern by large rocks. Kaija edged closer to the rocks and raised her head. She nearly cried aloud when she saw Luuka and Tarin a short distance away from her. Tears blurred her eyes and she forced herself to stay still. She wasn't sure who else was in the cave.

Luuka looked tired, and in pain. He lay with his eyes closed, and for a moment Kaija thought he was dead. But then she saw the gentle rise and fall of his breath, and the tight feeling around her own chest eased.

Tarin sat with his back to Luuka. He turned his head to speak to him, and Luuka roused slightly, but neither saw Kaija hiding in the rocks. She shifted her feet, making no sound, but then she paused. What had she heard? A movement? A sound? No, it was the feeling of being watched . . .

The hairs on her scalp and along her arms prickled, and slowly, ever so slowly, she turned to face the shadows. Something was there, lurking. Two orange eyes glowed with cold fire. Kaija's breath froze in her throat as the shadow moved. A low growl, lips pulled back in a snarl. A wolf!

She felt the blood drain from her face.

A wolf! And she had no weapon. She could almost feel the savage teeth ripping her throat. Maybe if she closed her eyes, it would be fast.

But she couldn't meet her death in darkness. If she was to die, she wanted to meet her fate with her eyes open. She wanted to see the Spirits who came for her.

The wolf moved forward, ears flat against its head, fur

bristling and tail straight out. Two small pups wound around its legs, but the wolf paid them no attention. Its eyes focused on Kaija and it moved towards her.

Life returned to Kaija's frozen limbs, and she took a step backwards, resisting the urge to run. Her foot wobbled on a rock, and she lost balance. She cried out as she sat down hard on the rocky ground. Air rushed from her lungs. She lay helpless, waiting for the wolf to pounce.

'Kaija?' Luuka's voice was weak, but she heard his call.

'O . . . over here,' she stammered, keeping her eyes on the wolf. 'There's . . . there's a . . . a wolf . . .'

'Stay still,' Luuka said. 'Can you see the tie around her neck?'

Kaija swallowed and dragged her eyes from the gaze of the wolf. Now that Luuka had pointed it out to her, she could see the rope wrapped around the wolf's neck. It strained tight.

'She's tied up,' said Luuka. 'She won't hurt you. Just move slowly around the edge of the cave.'

Kaija wet her dry lips and struggled to her feet. The wolf growled low in her throat, but made no attempt to attack. The orange eyes followed her as she edged carefully around the rocks, to Luuka and Tarin on the other side.

'Luuka! Oh, Luuka!' Kaija sobbed and threw her arms around him.

'Don't let the Spirit Keeper see you.' Tarin twisted his head around to them.

'Tarin!' Kaija embraced Tarin fiercely, then sat back on her heels and wiped her eyes. 'We have to get out of here.' She pulled her flint knife from her belt and cut their ties. Tarin rubbed his burning wrists and helped Luuka to his feet.

'The wolves, too.' Luuka clutched his ribs. 'We have to save them.'

'Are you mad?' Kaija gasped.

'I'm not leaving without them.' Luuka knelt before the she-wolf and reached his hand towards her.

'He is mad,' Kaija whispered. Tarin held his breath, but the wolf didn't attack. She sniffed Luuka's hand and whimpered, then reached forward to lick his fingertips. Luuka smiled and let his hand rest in the thick, blood-stained fur around her neck. He stroked her head and scratched behind her ears. The pups whimpered and tried to climb into his lap.

'Give me the knife,' Luuka said, his eyes never leaving the wolf's gaze.

Kaija stood frozen to the spot, her hands hanging limply by her side. Tarin grabbed the knife from her. 'Here.'

Luuka stared into the eyes of the wolf, as though mesmerised. One of the pups whimpered and jumped up at its mother, startling them all. Luuka shook his head and cut through her bindings. The wolf stood and shook herself. She flung back her head and howled, but this time it was a howl of triumph, instead of pain and hopelessness.

'Tarin, take this!' Luuka handed him a bundle of grey fur, pushing the other pup down into his own coat. Tarin had no time to think. He pushed the wolf pup down, aware of the warmth of its tiny body.

'Hurry!' Kaija hopped from one foot to the other. She pushed the boys towards the tunnel.

'Where are my little worms?' A voice drifted down into the cave, freezing them in horror. A cascade of rocks echoed around the chamber. 'What are you up to, my little worms?'

'She's in the secret tunnel!' Kaija's voice squeaked. 'We're trapped.'

Tarin spun around, searching the cave. 'We can hide.'

'There's nowhere to hide,' Luuka said. 'We just have to leave by the front entrance. It's our only chance.' He clutched the wolf pup to his chest and pushed Kaija ahead of him.

'I can hear you, dirty little worms. I know you're up to something.' The Spirit Keeper's voice was louder now. She groaned and strained as she made her way down the tunnel, closer and closer.

A deep growl rumbled in the she-wolf's throat. Her eyes

blazed and the fur rose along her back.

'Wolf! Follow me.' Luuka's voice was low and calm. He made small noises, calling to the animal. 'See? Your baby is here. He's safe with me. Come, you must come.'

'Luuka, come on!' Kaija called desperately to her brother as they ran for the entrance.

'Worms! Little worms! I'm going to mash your bones and suck the marrow.'

'Wolf! Come.' Luuka's voice rose in despair. 'Please . . .'

'I have to go back for him,' Kaija said, looking frantically behind her.

'No!' Tarin grabbed her arm and she struggled against him.

'Let me go,' she hissed furiously. 'I have to go back for my brother!'

Tarin shook her. 'He's coming. Luuka's coming.'

The wolf pup in his shirt stuck its head out and whimpered as Luuka and the she-wolf ran towards them out of the darkness. Tarin pushed it down and turned to run.

The entrance beckoned, promising freedom, but as they hurried towards it, a shadow fell over them.

Misfortune

Tarin stopped short at the sight of the stocky girl blocking their way. But to his surprise Kaija leapt forward and grabbed the girl's arms.

'Broda!' she said. 'Help us!'

'Give me my bead.' Broda glared at her. 'You promised.'

'Not now – your Spirit Keeper is right behind us,' Kaija hissed. She shook Broda in frustration. 'Help us, or you'll be caught too.'

Tarin held his breath as the two girls glared at one another, neither willing to give way. But then Luuka stepped into the light and Broda's gaze shifted to the wild animal at his side. Her face, which had been red with anger, turned white, and her eyes opened wide.

'The wolf!' She took a step back. The wolf growled and moved closer to the frightened girl.

'Stop it, Luuka,' Kaija said.

Luuka frowned at Broda, but he put his hand down to rest on the wolf's back, his fingers curled in her fur.

'She's one of them. She's Boar Clan.'

'But she can help us.'

Luuka scowled. He dropped to his knees and made soothing noises to the wolf. 'She can smell Boar Clan,' he muttered.

'We probably all smell like Boar Clan,' Kaija snapped. 'Broda, if you don't help us, we are all dead. You, too.'

Broda sniffed and thrust her jaw out. Then she nodded. 'This way. And keep low.'

She led them downhill by another path, out of sight of the huts but still towards the river. It was steeper than the main path, overgrown with ferns and treacherous with loose rocks. Tarin's leg ached, but he clenched his teeth and willed it to stay strong. With each step, agony lanced through him. His ankle turned on one of the rocks, and Broda hissed at him to keep quiet. She paused halfway down to peer through the branches.

All was quiet in the camp. A lone girl sat by the cooking fire, and a muddy child played by the river's edge. Of the men and women of Boar Clan, there was no sign.

'Where is everyone?' Tarin leaned forward. A twig

snapped under his feet and Broda pushed him back angrily.

'All are preparing for the Spirit Ceremony,' she said. 'This is your chance. When you get to the river, turn downstream. If you can reach Deer Clan territory by nightfall, you'll be safe. If not . . .' She shrugged, and a smile lifted the corners of her mouth. Tarin didn't like the gleam in her eyes. He wanted to ask more questions, when a scream shattered the quiet. It was high-pitched and furious. A flock of startled birds took to the sky, momentarily blocking the sun.

'Hela!' Broda's face paled. 'She's reached the main cave.'

'Run!' Kaija said.

'Wait!' Broda grabbed for Kaija's arm. 'My bead!'

But Kaija was already flying down the cliff path, followed by Luuka and Tarin.

Fear spurred Tarin on. His leg twisted beneath him, but still he ran. Rocks slipped under his feet, his knees hit the ground. Kaija grabbed him by the arm and hauled him up. Branches slapped his face and tore his clothes. Behind him, he was aware of Luuka's pained gasps.

'Kaija! I . . . can't . . . make . . . it . . .' The words seared Tarin's lungs as he forced them out. He felt as though small slivers of flint lined his throat, digging deeper with each breath. His leg had no strength and it collapsed beneath him.

'You have to!' Kaija grabbed him by the front of his

beaska and lifted him to his feet. She shook him, and he saw his own fear reflected in her eyes. 'You have to, Tarin. You can do it.' Her voice was softer this time . . . pleading.

Tarin gripped his lips together and nodded.

More screams filled the air. Raw, hateful. The screams of a savage animal.

Kaija's face went white. She urged her brother on, helping him. He clutched his ribs, his mouth a grim line, sweat running down his face. The wolf still ran at his side, but her chest was heaving and her tail was tucked between her legs. She flinched and snarled as another scream burst from the cave behind them. Tarin heard answering cries – the shouts of men and running feet.

'Down!' he hissed. He stooped low and pulled Kaija and Luuka into the overhanging branches of an old willow.

Boar Clan hunters clutching spears rushed past them towards the cave.

'The coracles!' said Kaija, pointing. 'They're right there.'

Two small boats were pulled up onto the riverbank. A third bobbed in the current, tied with a leather thong. The girl minding the fire stood in the middle of the camp, the muddy child clasped in her arms, but her attention was on the cave and the screams of the Spirit Keeper. Tarin wanted to cover his ears and cower in the mud, but they had only seconds to act.

'Go!' he said. 'Go! Go! Go!' He pushed Kaija ahead of him and turned to give his shoulder to Luuka. The River Clan boy was in pain. His eyes were glazed and he breathed in short, sharp gasps. Luuka leaned heavily on Tarin's shoulder and together they stumbled towards the coracles.

Spirit of Owl . . . give me strength.

The she-wolf hurried ahead of him and he felt the wolf pup squirm inside his shirt.

Spirit of Mammoth . . . give us courage . . .

Kaija waded out into the water towards the third coracle and unlooped its tether. She pushed the boat towards the boys as they reached the water's edge.

'Where's the knife?' Tarin asked, propping Luuka against one of the upturned boats on the riverbank. Luuka pressed his lips together and pulled the knife from his belt. With a mighty swipe, Tarin brought the blade down sharply, slicing the aurochs hide hull of the boat. But the hide was thick and tough. Again he slashed, and again, finally ripping the skin apart.

'They are there! I see them!'

Tarin, Luuka and Kaija looked up towards the mouth of the cave. The Spirit Keeper stood with her arms raised in the air, her staff held over her head.

'Get them! Bring them to me! I want to rip the beating hearts from their bodies.'

Panic seized Tarin. His ears filled with the sound of the Spirit Keeper's screams and the sound of his own blood pounding through his veins. Savagely he slashed the other boat, unaware the knife blade was cutting into his hand. He saw Kaija shouting – her mouth open, her eyes wild – but he couldn't hear her above the chaotic throbbing in his head.

He felt the knife pass through the hide, but as it did he fumbled and it fell into the thick mud at the water's edge. Before Tarin could reach for it, he heard Luuka shouting, 'Look out!'

Durk was rushing towards them, fury twisting his face. He clasped a spear in his hand and he drew back, ready to launch it towards the boys. Tarin turned to stone. He couldn't move. He couldn't run. He saw Durk's muscles tense, his eyes narrowed, focused on his target. His feet pounded as he charged forward, a mighty bison. The image of the spear slicing through the practice bag flashed through Tarin's mind, and he imagined his own stomach sliced open, his insides spilling into the mud at his feet.

But before Durk could make his cast, a snarling blur of grey fur launched itself towards him. The she-wolf bit hard into his arm, her teeth sinking through Durk's leather shirt and into his flesh. She held on, even as Durk dropped his spear with a scream and tried to pull his arm away from her. The wolf dug her teeth deeper and shook her head from side to side. Durk's blood flowed, warm and red.

'Luuka! Get in the boat!'

Kaija's voice broke Tarin's trance. Noises crowded him. Kaija screaming. The Spirit Keeper screaming. The snarling wolf ripping Durk's flesh.

'Wolf! Leave him! Stop! Wolf!'

Luuka lunged for the frenzied animal, trying to pull her away. Durk was a strong man, and with his free arm he pounded the weakened wolf in the ribs. He gouged her eyes and wrestled her to the ground.

'Luuka, they are coming!' Kaija screamed, as the rest of Boar Clan poured down the path from the cave.

'Wolf!' Luuka grabbed hold of the wolf, and tried to pull her off Durk, but the tortured animal could no longer tell friend from foe. As Luuka wrapped his arms around her, she turned and sank her teeth into his hand.

It was the chance Durk needed. He picked up a spear with his good arm and plunged it into the wolf's neck. Red, hot blood spurted out, covering them both. The wolf released Luuka and turned towards Durk with a final snarl. Then her body went limp and the fire in her eyes died. Durk lay back, his eyes closed, his chest rising and falling. Blood flowed from his arm.

'No!' Luuka fell forward over the fallen animal. He buried his face in her bloody fur.

'Luuka!' Tarin's throat felt raw. He grabbed Luuka and shook him.

Tears streamed down Luuka's face. 'She didn't mean it. She was just defending herself.' He held his arm against his chest, staining his *beaska* red.

'We have to go. Now!' Tarin pulled Luuka to his feet and forced him towards the boat.

Spirit of Horse . . . give us speed.

He pushed Luuka into the boat and scrambled in after him. Kaija was knee-deep in the river, unwinding the tether from a semi-submerged tree. Durk raised himself on one elbow and cast a spear towards them, but his throw was weak and splashed harmlessly in the water.

'Hurry!' Tarin reached out of the coracle towards Kaija.

Durk staggered to one knee and readied himself for another cast, but before he could, Broda rushed forward and hit him on the side of the head with a tree branch. The big man collapsed, facedown in the mud.

Tarin reached for Kaija's arms and hauled her into the coracle. The little boat listed to one side, but it stayed afloat.

'Give me my beads!' Broda caught the floating tether and pulled back on it. Her feet dug deep into the mud and her shoulders strained against the current that wanted to carry the little boat away. 'You promised.'

'Broda, let go of the rope!' Kaija screamed. 'You'll tip us.'

'My beads!'

Kaija hissed in frustration but she knew Broda was right. It was only because of the Boar Clan girl that they were escaping. She ripped a small pouch from around her waist. 'Here!' She tossed the pouch towards the Boar Clan girl. 'You can have them all – you've earned them.'

Broda let go of the tether and caught the pouch as it sailed through the air. Her lips curved in a smile of triumph.

Kaija leaned towards her, her voice urgent. 'Broda, come with us. You'll be in trouble for helping us.'

But Broda shook her head and clutched the pouch. The little boat, free at last, spun around as the river current picked it up.

'They attacked Durk!' Broda's voice carried across the water. 'They're getting away!'

Tarin ducked as a spear splashed into the water next to him. The hunters were in range. He grabbed one of the deer antler paddles and plunged it into the water. Slowly, the boat moved away from the riverbank.

'Get down!' he cried. Another spear came perilously close to the coracle. The little boat was now in the middle of the river, but Tarin knew the spear throwers would still reach them.

'Paddle deeper, Tarin! Don't just splash the water!' Kaija grabbed the other paddle and showed him how to manage the little boat. 'We have to get further downstream.'

Tarin tried to copy the River Clan girl's movements, and the coracle picked up speed. He glanced at Luuka, lying on the bottom of the boat. The boy's face was white and his arm was still bleeding.

'Don't let Ristak sleep,' Old Mother had said. 'If he sleeps, the Spirits will think he is ready to journey with them to the Spirit World. You have to keep him awake, Tarin.' But the pain had been too much, and Old Mother had brewed the special tea to help Ristak on his journey.

'Don't let him sleep,' Tarin urged Kaija.

'I'm fine,' Luuka groaned, and pushed himself upright. 'Tarin, give me that paddle before you drown us.'

Tarin turned to pass the paddle, but as he did, he saw a blur of movement out of the corner of his eye. Even as he opened his mouth to yell, the spear hurtled towards the boat and pierced Kaija in the shoulder.

The impact threw her backwards, and Kaija fell.

A Desperate
Flight

'Kaija!' Luuka dropped the paddle and reached for his sister.

Tarin turned to search the riverbank. There, high on the cliff, he saw the hunter. He thought it was the girl, Farla, but he couldn't be certain.

The hunter stood a moment, a spear thrower in her hand, then she turned and disappeared into the forest as the river swept the little coracle away.

Tarin turned his attention back to Kaija. She lay on the bottom of the boat, the spear still stuck in her shoulder. Blood oozed from the wound and her lips were white.

Luuka had eased a hand beneath her head. 'Kaija, speak to me,' he said. 'Are you alive?'

Kaija stirred. 'No,' she said, and groaned.

Tarin stared at her in consternation. 'You're not a Spirit.

Spirits don't bleed. At least, I don't think they do.'

Kaija drew a shuddering breath and tried to smile at them. 'I'm alive,' she said. 'We need mistletoe and golden flower to staunch the bleeding, but we don't have either of them.' Her voice rose in panic. 'And you need to pull the spear out.'

Tarin chewed his lip. He wasn't sure what to do. 'Luuka? Can you reach into my pack? See what you can find to stop the bleeding.' The front of Tarin's *beaska* wriggled and a wolf pup stuck out his head. He pulled the pup out and it huddled miserably in the bottom of the boat.

Kaija groaned as Luuka unstrapped the pack from her back. He struggled with the lacings and drew his breath in sharply.

'How are your ribs?' Tarin asked him.

'Not good.' Luuka grimaced as he dug into the pack. 'But I'll live.'

'Both of you need medicine.' Tarin ran his hand through his hair and studied the riverbank as the boat floated downstream. 'I don't know where we are. We need to dock, but what if Boar Clan is following? We can't risk it yet.'

Luuka nodded. The pup down the front of his *beaska* wriggled out and licked the wound on his hand. The bleeding had slowed, but the puncture wounds on his hand and forearm were deep.

'I think he's sorry,' Luuka murmured with a slight smile. He pulled Tarin's fox furs from the bag. 'Can we use these?'

'Of course.' Tarin pulled sharply at the pelts, and the sinew holding them together ripped apart. One of them he passed to Luuka to wrap around his forearm where the deepest wounds were.

Tarin wished Old Mother were here with her special bag of dried and fresh herbs, soft strips of rabbit skin bandages, and specially carved bones to ward off the evil Spirits of sickness. But she wasn't. He clasped his owl pendant in his hands.

Spirit of Owl, help me. Help us.

He had seen spear wounds before, but then Kalle or one of the men had been there to pull the spear from the wound. Once, Kalle had pulled a spear from his own shoulder. He had laughed about it, and refused Old Mother's golden flower tea, but by nightfall his face was white and he sweated as though he were sitting next to the coals in one of the clan's sweat baths. Aila told him to lie down and made sure he drank the tea. Then he slept for a whole night and the next day as well.

Tarin looked down at Kaija and realised she was watching him. She nodded as if she could read his thoughts.

'You have to pull the spear out, Tarin. Be quick. Be strong.' Her voice trailed away and she closed her eyes.

For a moment, Tarin thought she had fainted, but then she reached a hand towards the wolf pups. They licked her fingers and curled into furry balls next to her. A shudder shook her body. 'Just do it, Tarin. Don't worry about the pain.'

'I can try, but I'm afraid I don't have the strength,' said Luuka.

'I can do it,' Tarin said, and he was surprised that his voice didn't tremble. He sounded braver than he felt. He wiped his sweaty hands down his leggings and gripped the spear. He pulled slightly, testing it. Kaija groaned and squeezed her eyes shut. She clasped Luuka's uninjured hand.

Tarin wet his lips. 'Luuka, I'll pull the spear. You be ready to staunch the blood.' Luuka nodded and looked grim.

Tarin gripped the spear shaft firmly. And pulled.

Kaija cried out. With the sound of tearing flesh, the spear shaft came loose. Luuka pressed the furs down over the bleeding wound.

'That's . . . good.' Kaija shuddered and then pressed her lips tightly together. Her whole body started to shake. 'Luuka . . . stop my Spirit from bleeding away.'

Luuka bunched the furs tighter.

Tarin stared at the spear still clasped in his hands. It was short, like all the Boar Clan spears, and tipped with bone – a long, thin sliver now stained with Kaija's blood.

He shuddered and dropped the spear.

The river was becoming more turbulent. White water appeared ahead, foaming around hidden rocks and debris. The boys had no choice but to grab the paddles and try to steer the coracle away from the churning water.

'When we find calmer water we can clean the wound and ...' Tarin's voice trailed away. 'Spirit of Owl, watch over us.'

'He will,' said Luuka, and he narrowed his eyes and concentrated on keeping their little craft afloat. Light was fading, and Tarin shook from exhaustion. Luuka's arm was red and swollen, a sure sign that evil Spirits were infecting the wound. Kaija was pale and slept fitfully.

Don't let Ristak sleep ...

Tarin's head snapped up and he realised he had dozed. They were still floating downriver, carried along by the current. He had no idea where the river led, or how far they had travelled. He searched the riverbank, but soon felt his eyes drooping again. He was so tired. All he wanted to do was sleep, just for a little while.

Kaija moaned. Her lips were dry and her face wet with sweat. Tarin scooped up a handful of water and washed her face. She licked the water and her eyes opened.

'Retu?' She stared at Tarin, then her eyelids fluttered shut and her breathing deepened.

Tarin looked up at the sky. They couldn't stay on the river in the dark – it was too dangerous. They could collide with rocks or logs, or be swept over rapids.

'Luuka? Do you know where we are?'

Luuka shook his head. He was paddling with his left hand now, holding his right arm stiff to his side. His eyes were dark with pain. Tarin took up the other paddle and helped him coax the boat closer to the riverbank.

Large, graceful willows trailed their greenery in the water. Broad-leaved reedmace and tall bulrushes edged the bank. The current slowed, and the boys found it easier to manoeuvre the craft. Long shadows rippled in the water as they finally chose a place to dock. A few soft snowflakes fell, promising a heavier fall overnight.

It was dim under the willow branches, and Tarin felt safe from prying eyes. He slipped over the side of the coracle, landing knee-deep in water and soft mud. Ice crusted around the trailing willow roots, crunching as the boat slid close. One of the pups landed in the water with a splash. Tarin reached for it, but it was already pulling itself up the riverbank. It shook its small body, sending a shower of water over him. In the coracle, its litter mate whimpered and whined, unwilling to brave the cold water.

'You're the smart one, aren't you?' Tarin murmured. 'Pass it here.'

'Her,' said Luuka, and passed her over. The pup shook her paws indignantly as Tarin put her down next to her brother, who pounced and wrestled her to the ground. The falling snowflakes distracted him, and he began to chase them in a vain attempt to catch one of the falling flakes. The riverbank was slippery with mud and dirty snow. The snow was falling faster now, covering the ground.

'If we can get the boat out of the water, then tip it over, we could use it as a shelter,' Luuka said.

Tarin glanced up at the thickening snow and nodded. Together, they pushed and pulled the coracle up the slippery slope. The jerky movement woke Kaija and they helped her out of the boat. She lay back against a rock, her face white and strained.

'We need a fire,' said Tarin. 'I think we're far enough away from Boar Clan . . .'

'How far do you think we came?' Kaija murmured.

Tarin shook his head. He didn't know. He had tried to keep track of the twists and turns of the river, but the land around here was too unfamiliar. He hoped it was still familiar to Kaija and she still knew the way to the Mother's Mountain. He gathered dry wood and used the last of his tinder to light the fire. He struck the stones confidently, creating a strong, bright spark.

'What did you do?' Luuka jumped to his feet.

Tarin looked at him in surprise. 'What do you mean? What's wrong?'

Brother and sister stared at Tarin with fearful eyes.

'The fire!' croaked Kaija. 'How did you do that? Is that ... magic?'

Tarin looked down at the rocks in his hands, puzzled. 'There's no magic. I just used the firestones.' A thought came to him. 'Do you mean you've never seen a firestone?' He held the stones out towards them.

'Do they burn?' Luuka reached for them. 'They are cold!'

'Show me.' Kaija's voice was weak, but she examined the stones with interest. 'This is flint.'

'That's right.' Tarin nodded. He took the stones back and showed them the striking movement. 'The flint draws the spark from the firestone.' Then he scratched his nose and looked carefully at the stones himself. 'Maybe it is magic. On the steppes, we have little wood to burn. We burn dried dung and shaved mammoth bones. The stones are how we always light our fires.'

'You mean, you have more of these magic stones?' Luuka asked.

'We find them along the riverbanks,' said Tarin. 'Especially after the Spring rains. But usually we never let our fires go out. The stones are used for travelling.'

'River Clan uses a wood platform and birch drill. But

it takes a long time,' murmured Kaija. A shiver shook her body and she held her hands out to the warming flames.

Tarin opened his pouch and examined the small packet of dried willowbark. There wasn't much left, but here by the riverbank, willowbark grew in profusion. He reached for the flint knife to strip some bark, then realised he no longer had it. With a groan, he remembered dropping the knife in the river during their escape.

'This is a good fire, Tarin,' Kaija said, but she sounded weak and tired.

We all need rest and food and a cup of hot tea, Tarin thought. His leg and shoulders ached. He was covered in blood. In the gathering gloom, each sound seemed louder, and each shadow more foreboding. Tarin found himself jumping at everything. They had hardly any food. There were three strips of dried reindeer meat left from the Offering, and one salmon cake, as well as a handful of dried blueberries and mushrooms. He broke one of the reindeer strips in half and waved it at the wolf pups.

'This is all I have to give you. And I'm not chewing it up for you. You're going to have to learn to eat it.' He gave half a strip to each pup and smiled as they sniffed the unfamiliar food.

'Go ahead. It's tastier than that wolverine.' He passed the other strips to Luuka and Kaija, as well as a few of the berries and mushrooms, but Kaija passed hers back to him.

'I don't think I can eat,' she said. 'I'm so tired.'

Tarin didn't feel like eating either – his stomach was tied in knots of worry. But he sipped some tea and was glad of the warmth.

The last light dimmed. Somewhere, Tarin thought he heard an owl hoot. He stirred the flames and watched them burn more brilliantly for a moment. They needed to clean their wounds, but a great weariness weighed him down. The wolf pups curled into balls, snuggling next to him. He could feel their warmth through his leggings and damp *beaska*. Luuka and Kaija both closed their eyes and fell into uneasy sleeps. Tarin dozed fitfully, his brief snatches of sleep filled with vivid dreams – images of Hela, and the now-familiar dream of the mammoths moving further and further away from him.

But then the dream changed.

The herd of mammoths were vague grey shadows, blanketed in thick mist.

'Mother,' the little one cried out, and the female mammoth stopped and looked back at him.

'Tarin, my son.' It was his mother's voice. But he could not reach her over the chasm.

'You must hurry, my son,' the mammoth said. She raised her trunk to catch the falling snow. 'The Ice Mother has come to us. She covers our land in snow and ice. Her anger freezes the plains.'

'Mother, help me.'

But the mammoth shook her shaggy head. 'I cannot help you, my child. And you cannot help us. Our journeys have parted. The Ice Mother searches for you. She reaches for you. Your time is so short.'

'Then what must I do?'

'You cannot think like Mammoth any more, pushing and fighting against the Ice Mother. The glacier lands are too far away. You will never reach them and you will surely die. Now, you must think like Wolf. See? I have brought Wolf to help you.' From the mist surrounding her, a large grey wolf appeared. His eyes glowed in the dimming light. The little mammoth knew a moment of fear as the wolf approached him, leaping easily over the chasm. The wolf came close, so close the little mammoth could feel the warmth of its breath and feel the touch of its fur. Its teeth gleamed long and white and it growled low in its throat.

The rest of the mammoth herd were no longer visible. The She-mammoth turned her head away, as though she were being called.

'Think like Wolf, my son. Find a place of safety. Hide from the Ice Mother. Do not try to fight her for her power is too great.'

'I cannot leave you, Mother!' Tarin screamed in his dream. 'I will not.'

'Then you shall die. You shall all die. If the Mother wishes, then we shall walk together once more, but now think only of your new clan, my son. Think now of the wolves. Find your place of safety, and quickly. Quickly, my son.'

And the She-mammoth turned and disappeared into the mist.

'Mother! Mother!' Tarin screamed, but the herd was gone, lost in the mist. The wolf lifted his head and howled, a long, mournful sound that tore Tarin's heart. He wanted to lift his own head and howl for his lost clan.

The feeling of loss stayed with him even when he woke.

Luuka was restless. He had a fever, and his arm was inflamed. Tarin bathed it in warm, clean water and helped him sip more willowbark tea. Luuka lay down again and stared at the fire, but Tarin could tell his arm still pained him.

Kaija also was restless. She would wake and cry out and her eyes were glazed. She cried out to people Tarin didn't know. He knew in her tortured dreams she was back home with her family.

'You cannot help them. Their Spirits do battle.' Old

Mother's voice echoed in his head.

Tarin closed his eyes, and for a moment, he, too, felt as though he were back home – back in Old Mother's earth-lodge, flickering firelight making the shadows dance, white mammoth bones gleaming, the constant rhythm of the drums, the sickly sweet scent of the burning herbs. And Ristak, his body broken by the horns of the mighty bison.

'The battle is fought, Spirit Protector against Spirit of Evil,' said Old Mother. 'The body grows hot. The eyes, they do not see. His Spirit prepares for the journey.'

'Old Mother, is there no hope?' Raisa raised her tear-stained face to the old healer.

'His totem protector is Spirit of Deer. Deer cannot win against Bison. There is no hope.'

Tarin remembered Raisa's wail of anguish. She fell to the floor next to Ristak, her tears falling on his body. Erik, her son, stood rigid in the shadows, unmoving. Old Father's chanting voice filled the earth-lodge.

'When the Spirits battle, we cannot help.'

But we can, thought Tarin, shaking his head to dispel the images. We must be able to. Surely the Spirits will listen, if we ask for their help. He clutched his pendant and thought about all the times Spirit of Owl had helped him.

'Spirit of Owl, I ask for your help,' he said. 'I ask that you help me to see clearly, to act wisely, to be strong in the face of my fear. With your help, I can face the dark Spirits, the bad Spirits that would harm us. Old Father says a Spirit Keeper must be strong and brave – stronger and braver than I will ever be – but I am alone here, without my clan, and I need your help. Please, Spirit of Owl, give me the courage to face the evil Spirits who would harm Luuka and Kaija. I will fight for them, for they are now my clan . . . my family.' He dropped his head.

I will not let the bad Spirits win. Wild Horse will win over savage Boar.

Walking with
the Spirits

Two years ago, in late spring ... Tarin's thoughts slipped back to that time. It was just before Mammoth Clan moved to their summer grounds. He and Taavo were supposed to be helping Old Mother scrape *pettu* from the pine trees – the soft layer between the bark and wood that the women would bake into small loaves of bread.

But Taavo had slipped away. Saiga Clan had joined Mammoth Clan to hunt a large herd of reindeer that were migrating north. Both clans wanted the warm pelts, meat and antlers for trading. Hoofs would be boiled to form thick glue. Stomachs, bladders and intestines washed and filled with water. Bones cracked, and the rich marrow scraped out, and everyone was looking forward to a special stew of fresh reindeer served with sweet lingonberries.

Jarmo and Markku had tracked the reindeer herd for days, and now all the hunters were in position. A temporary corral, made from twisted branches and old bones, blocked the reindeer's path, and from behind came a group carrying flaming torches and flapping skins to frighten the animals into a stampede.

But the hunters didn't know there was a pride of cave lions stalking the same herd.

Kalle saw them first – the giant felines, tawny-gold and larger than the fretful reindeer. He had moved away from the main group of hunters to head off an old doe. Her fur was coarse and she had little meat on her bones, but her reluctance to follow her younger sisters threatened to cause a stampede in the wrong direction.

A hungry lioness was watching the old doe. As Kalle moved forward, the lioness sprang – not at the doe, but at the larger meal, whose attention was distracted. Kalle had no time to raise his spear, but Isto, leader of Saiga Clan, and his son, Tarv, saw the danger and launched their spears. Isto's spear passed through the ribs of the lioness and she fell. But Tarv was a new hunter, young and inexperienced. His spear caught Kalle in the thigh and the spear head lodged there.

'Did you think this big lump was a bison to spear?' Isto thumped his son on the back. Tarv looked sick, but Kalle laughed and clasped Tarv by the shoulder.

'You will be a good leader one day, young one. You did not hesitate.'

I wanted to be on that hunt, Tarin thought. I could have helped herd the reindeer. Instead, he was left at camp and heard the tale from the others.

But he was there when they carried Kalle to Old Mother. He saw the five strong men it took to lift him, and he saw the worry in Old Mother's eyes . . . and the way her hand shook as she examined the wound. He heard the promises she made to the Spirits, if only they would let Kalle live.

'Tarin?' Kaija's voice was weak and fearful. In the flickering light of the fire, her eyes were sunken pools. She reached for Luuka, who was still tossing fretfully from side to side. 'He feels so hot.'

'It's the Spirits, fighting in his body,' Tarin said.

'Tarin? If the Spirits decide to take Luuka and me . . .' Kaija's voice trembled and she closed her eyes. Then she continued. 'If anything should happen, I want to thank you. For helping me rescue Luuka, and for being my friend.'

Tarin hesitated. He wanted to speak, to say something comforting to her, but he didn't know what.

'And,' Kaija said, 'I need to tell you what I have done.'

'Kaija, save your strength. Don't talk.' Tarin laid his hand briefly on her arm.

'But I told you things that ... were not true.' Her voice was fretful and weak. 'I need to tell you.'

Luuka cried out as a dream woke him. He stared at them with wild eyes, still caught in his nightmare.

Tarin squeezed Kaija's hand. 'We can talk when you and Luuka are well.'

Kaija nodded, but her eyes remained troubled.

Luuka's wounds were ugly and red. And it wasn't just the wounds from the wolf making him sick, Tarin thought, but the wound Boar Clan inflicted on his Spirit. Wounds to the Spirit were always the hardest to heal. Tarin passed him some tea. It was barely warm now but still good to drink.

'Thank you,' Luuka murmured. He didn't sleep again, but sat and stared into the flickering flames. His eyes were filled with pain and memories.

'Luuka, we need to clean your wounds,' Tarin said. As he spoke, he unpacked the rest of the parcels still in his backpack – the parcel of herbs Old Mother had sent for the Offering and the strips of soft buckskin given by Reindeer Hearth. Beneath his breath, he spoke softly to the Spirits.

'Forgive me,' he said. 'Forgive me for what I am doing. Do not punish Mammoth Clan because I have failed. Please, Great Mother, watch over them as they battle your sister, the Ice Mother. Know that I will still journey to your Mountain, and I will make my own Offering. I will offer to you everything I have, if you could please just save my clan, the old and the new.'

He opened the parcel and touched the small packets reverently. Each was tied differently; each had its own mark. Tarin heated more water and added a handful of dried herbs.

'That smells like bear's claw.' Kaija smiled weakly as she sniffed the steam curling upwards into the crisp air.

'And crushed horsetail.' Tarin watched the herbs steep. 'To bathe Luuka's arm and your shoulder.'

'They stop the blood, and clean it,' murmured Kaija. 'Tarin? Where did you get horsetail and bear's claw?'

Tarin didn't answer. He kept watching the herbs. He didn't want to look at Kaija. Not only because she would see the sadness in his eyes, but also the fear. He didn't want her to think him weak. He needed her to think he was strong, so that when he told her what he wanted to do, she would trust him.

'They're from the Offering, aren't they?' Kaija's voice was soft. 'Tarin, I'm so sorry.'

'It doesn't matter.' Tarin leant over the liquid and blew to cool it. 'You need my help.' He dipped a strip of buckskin into the liquid and thought of adding some soothing mayweed to the willowbark tea. 'Luuka, let me see your arm.'

They unwrapped the blood-soaked bandage and stared at the mangled flesh.

'Poor Wolf,' Luuka murmured. 'She didn't mean it.' Next to him, the wolf pups whimpered, but they didn't move.

'This will stop the blood flowing again,' Tarin said, bathing the wounds on his arm. 'You are now Chosen by Wolf, Luuka. Did you realise that?'

Luuka caught his breath sharply as the cleansing liquid washed away the dried blood, but he managed a smile. 'Chosen by Wolf,' he murmured as Kaija wrapped a clean, dry strip around his arm. 'A good totem.'

Tarin picked up the last packet of dried herbs and looked at it. It was wrapped in a small square of red dyed leather, and tied with a twist of Old Mother's own white hair. He brushed his fingers across it and thought of her – her frailty, and her strength. Her deep wisdom, and vast knowledge. Her happiness, and the well of great sorrow that Tarin knew was locked deep within her heart. She had seen so much, and suffered many losses during her long lifetime. She had seen fifty summers.

A movement broke his thoughts. The wolf pups yawned, turned in a circle, and resettled themselves next to Luuka with big sighs of contentment. There were no bad dreams disturbing their sleep.

'What is that?' Luuka asked. Tarin showed him the small packet and Luuka raised it to his nose to sniff. 'It smells familiar.'

'Mustara leaf.' Kaija drew her breath in sharply. 'What are you doing with mustara leaf, Tarin?'

Tarin stared at the dancing flames and rubbed the back of his neck. He breathed in the scent of the woodsmoke, so different to the sharper smell of burning bone. He closed his eyes and tried to capture the feeling of home – of sitting by the fire in the snug earth-lodge, smells of warming broth heavy on the air, the murmur of voices, perhaps the quiet chink of bone pieces as Eero and Ilmi played pick-em-up.

But he couldn't. It was too far away, and the feelings too raw.

'I need to speak to the Spirits,' Tarin said. 'A Spirit Keeper could drive the evil Spirits from your bodies with sage smoke and magic words. I don't have sage, and I don't know the right words, but with Owl's help, I will fight for you.'

'No!' Kaija said. 'I will not let you sacrifice yourself for me.'

'Or me,' said Luuka. He frowned at Tarin. 'If the Mother wishes us to live, we will. Horse will find a way to protect us.'

'But how can Horse fight against Boar? He cannot. He needs my help. Just as I need your help if we are to survive the Winter. No one of us can survive without the others. We need food, shelter, water, furs. Winter is here and we are weak and far from our homes.' Tarin took the packet back from Luuka and stroked the white hair tie. 'Old Mother dried the leaves herself. She hangs them upside down on a rack, away from the sun or any light. For a whole cycle of seasons she dries them, and then crushes them to powder and mixes them with black cherry . . .'

Tarin's voice faded. He watched Kaija as she chewed her lip and stared at the ground in front of her. She was the daughter of a healer. She would know all about mustara, the pretty low-growing shrub with the creamy flowers. Tea made from the carefully dried roots would bring on endless sleep, but the leaves, properly treated, were gentler. The flowers themselves, with their hearts of deeper orange, caused extreme pain and wild hallucinations, and were deadly.

'Your Old Mother dried them herself?'

'I wouldn't trust them if she hadn't.' Tarin's fingers brushed the packet again. 'See? She has sealed them with her own hair.'

Kaija took the packet from him and examined it. Another tremor shook her body, and she shivered. 'I grow cold again.'

'The fever won't leave you until the Spirits end their battle.'

'Why do you need the tea?' Kaija's eyes were worried.

'It is how the Mammutti Spirit Keepers enter the Spirit World,' said Tarin. 'That's what Valo told me.'

Only a very powerful Spirit Keeper can enter the Spirit

World without the tea, Tarin Twisted Leg. Even with the tea, it is a dangerous journey — one you will never be brave enough or strong enough to make.

But I must try, Tarin thought. He traced the mark of Owl on his pendant and frowned.

'All my life I have sent my thanks and my pleas to Owl and Mammoth, but how do I know they can hear me now, so far away from my home? Maybe my voice is too soft to be heard. That's why I must enter their world, and speak to them face to face. You are weak from your wounds. You cannot fight your battle by yourself, but I can help you. I can fight the bad Spirits for you, just as Valo Spirit Keeper would fight for me if I were home.'

Kaija shook her head. 'I don't like it. What if you don't wake up?'

'Then you and Luuka still have each other.' Tarin held his hand out for the packet. 'I can do this, Kaija. Trust me, like I trust you.'

Kaija bit her lip. 'Luuka, don't let him.'

Luuka stared at the fire and didn't speak for a long time.

'It is his decision,' he said finally. 'How can I help?'

'Just watch over Kaija,' said Tarin. 'If the Spirits are too strong, or if I don't wake . . .' He stopped and drew a deep breath. 'Her wound will need bathing and re-dressing tomorrow. You need to find shelter and food.'

Luuka grasped Tarin's shoulder. 'You will wake. And you will succeed. The Spirits will hear you. Tomorrow we will begin a new journey and find that shelter together.'

Tarin made the tea the way Old Mother had taught him. The water, not too hot. The leaves, enough to fit in the palm of his hand, then half taken away to please the Spirits. There was no Spirit Keeper there to help, so Tarin said the special words himself. He hoped the Spirits would be pleased with them.

'Ancient Spirits,
Spirit of Ice, Spirit of Rain, Spirit of Rock.
You who formed the land.
Blessed Spirit, Earth Mother,
You who gave us life.
Protector Spirits,
Spirit of Owl, Wolf and Horse.
Protect your children.'

He finished saying the words and threw the herbs into the water. The water bubbled upwards, but it didn't spill.

'It will be bitter,' Kaija said.

Tarin nodded. He knew the taste well. It was the tea Old Mother gave him to take the spirit from his body while she healed his leg. He tipped half into his cup and stared down at the dark liquid. Steam rose, curling up into the night sky. Tarin shivered. When Old Mother gave him the tea, she made sure it was not too strong – not strong enough to break the barrier between their world and the Spirit World. But Tarin didn't know how to test for strength. He breathed in the steam. It smelled familiar. It looked familiar.

But what if he didn't wake?

His glance fell on Kaija. She was shivering again, her eyes full of fear. Her Spirit of Horse was losing her battle. And Luuka? His face was grim and pain-filled. His arm hung uselessly by his side, his fingertips just brushing the wolf pups as they slept.

I have to do this.

Tarin gripped the cup and took a deep breath. He licked his dry lips. But still he sat there, cross-legged by the fire, and stared down into the tea.

The tickle started at the base of his skull, where it always did. First, the little fine hairs on his neck rose, then his whole scalp tingled. It was always the same before one of his dreams – that feeling of something gentle yet fire-hot brushing against his skin, warning him. His hearing would become keener, his eyesight sharper, and his head felt as though it were too small to contain all the dreams and visions pressing against him.

Sometimes all he felt was pain. It travelled from behind

his eyes and outwards to every part of his body. Then all he would see was a world awash in lights and colours, so he would squeeze his eyes shut again and call on Owl to take the dreams away. Owl would take him up into the sky, and together they would fly free over the plains. That was when Old Mother would heal his leg, twisting it this way and that to drive the bad Spirits away.

Owl, hear me!

And Owl answered him, as he always did, as he always would. Owl lifted him upwards on wings that were strong and free.

'Tarin?'

He heard Luuka's voice from a long way away, but he was flying now with Owl and had no words for the River Clan boy. Tarin wheeled in the sky to circle over the little camp huddled by the side of the river. Snow was falling softly, but their fire was warm and welcoming. He swooped low over Luuka, and the boy turned his head sharply, as though he had heard the whisper of wings above his head. Kaija groaned in her fever-induced sleep. Her spirit was fighting, but even Horse cannot run forever.

Then the camp was gone, and Tarin found himself in the depths of a thick forest. Here, daylight couldn't penetrate the deep-green foliage, and the snow barely filtered through the thick canopy overhead.

He was no longer flying with Owl. Now, he padded through the forest on four legs, his keen nose picking out the scent of the forest animals, his grey fur blending with the darkness so that he was invisible.

There was a scent, a stinking, pungent scent, worrying him. He growled low in his throat and the hackles on his back rose. It was the scent of Boar. The wolf's muzzle wrinkled. Moonlight gleamed on white fangs. Boar was still in the forest – Wolf's forest – and Wolf was not happy.

Then another scent crossed him and he followed. It was the scent of the two humans Owl had seen camped by the river. Their Spirits were sick, blanketed in grey mist. Wolf found them now in a clearing of the forest. He growled at the greyness around them, and it shifted like long grass in the wind. Wolf flung back his head and howled, calling for more wolves to join him. In the distance, another wolf answered, then another. The forest wolves came fast and silent.

The greyness shifted again. Wolf paced from side to side, snarling. He lunged forward, snapping at the greyness, driving it backward into the forest, where the trees would swallow it forever.

This was Wolf's forest. No place for intruders.

The boy stirred in his sleep. The shadow lifted from his dreams. He was marked by Wolf, and strong. Horse welcomed Wolf.

But the girl . . .

Wolf's keen nose picked up the odour of festering sickness. The greyness was within her, and would not leave. Wolf circled her, snarling. The Boar scent was strong. It fed the growing darkness. Horse was lost and trapped, unable to help. Wolf lunged towards her and bit the wound on her shoulder. That was where the darkness was. He tasted Boar, sour and vicious. The poison was killing her, and like a dream within a dream, Wolf saw the boy once more pull the spear from her shoulder. It was a savage spear, tipped with bone, long and sharp. Wolf saw the girl, Farla, sitting by the river, grinding the bone between two flat stones. She held it up to the light and smiled. Then she took a flint knife and notched the edges, creating small hooks to tear the flesh of her prey.

Wolf looked at the spear, still clasped in the boy's hand, the tip red with blood, jagged and broken, and suddenly, Wolf understood. When the boy had pulled the spear from her shoulder, a small sliver of bone remained. That was the smell of Boar. That's what was destroying the girl's Spirit.

Wolf flung his head back and howled. Around him, the forest echoed with the answering howls of his clan. The two humans woke and looked around them fearfully.

You have no reason to fear, Wolf wanted to tell them. You are Clan. You are Wolf, too.

The wolf pups whimpered and tried to lift their heads to howl, soft mewls lost in the louder clamour of the forest wolves. Luuka hushed them and eased their fears. He felt Kaija's forehead and his frown deepened.

'Tarin! She grows worse!' a voice called.

And Tarin-wolf was once more running through the forest, his forest, towards the river.

Wolf Clan

'Tarin!' Luuka shook his shoulder. 'If you are going to drink that tea, drink it now. Kaija needs your help.'

The vision of the forest faded from Tarin's mind, but the feeling of running through the thick woods on four legs stayed with him so strongly that he looked down at his own two legs in confusion.

'What?' he said, and even to his own ears, his voice sounded vague and far away. And his hands were still clasped around the cup of tea. He frowned at the muddy liquid still there. He didn't understand.

'Tarin!' Luuka's voice was urgent. Kaija was agitated. Her eyes were open, but glazed with fever. Sweat ran down her face.

'I'm so c . . . cold.' Her teeth chattered together.

Tarin put the tea down and clasped her hands in his. Hers were burning hot.

'Kaija! Listen to me.' He tried to calm her. 'There is a piece of the spear head caught in your wound.'

Kaija stopped fighting him and tried to listen. 'What?'

'How do you know?' Luuka asked.

'Spirit of Wolf showed me,' Tarin said. 'I . . .' He stopped, unsure how to explain what had happened to him.

'You talked with the Spirits?' Luuka stared at him.

Tarin drew a deep breath. He hadn't just talked with the Spirits – he had been one of them. He had been Spirit of Wolf. He had seen and smelled and sensed as Wolf. He had run on four paws, low to the ground. He had lifted his head and howled to the wolf brothers he knew were all around him. But he couldn't explain that to Luuka. He couldn't explain it to himself.

Later, maybe, when Kaija was out of danger, then he would sit and think about what he had experienced. For now, Kaija's life was the most important thing for him to think about, and he knew now how to save her.

'I talked with the Spirits.' He gripped Kaija's hands. 'I can help you, but it will hurt. The fever won't leave you until the spear head is taken out and your wound can heal.'

'I know.' The healer's daughter shuddered and reached a tentative hand to her shoulder. 'You must cut the wound larger . . .' Another shiver shook her body.

Tarin nodded. 'There is still tea here. Will you drink it?

It will help to take away the pain.'

'No.' Kaija shook her head. 'I will hold still.'

'You can't, Kaija. You're already shivering so much.' Luuka frowned at her.

'Then you hold me, while Tarin cuts.'

Luuka raked his good hand through his hair. 'I don't have two arms to hold you with. Why are you so stubborn? It will be less painful if you drink the tea.'

Tears rolled down Kaija's cheeks. 'Why can't you believe me. I said I can hold still.'

'Kaija.' Tarin gripped her hand. 'You may think you can stay still, but what if I have to dig the bone out? You will move, and I may cause you more injury.'

Kaija sobbed quietly while the two boys frowned at her. One of the wolf pups nuzzled her hand and licked her fingertips. She drew in a shaky breath.

'You are right.' She brushed the tears from her face. 'The smell of the tea – it reminds me of our last days in River Clan.' Her fingers sank into the wolf pup's fur and she dropped her shoulders. 'If I were alone, I would say to the Spirits – here I am, come and take me. But I'm not alone.'

'Never alone.' Luuka hugged his sister.

'Never alone,' Tarin said. He held the cup towards her.

'Help me, Luuka. My hand shakes.'

'Ready?' Luuka asked.

'Ready,' she said, and he held the cup to her lips.

Kaija gagged as the liquid tipped down her throat. She passed the empty cup back to Tarin. Soon, she would sleep, and feel no pain, but she knew the pain would be there for her when she woke. If she woke.

'Tarin? Talk to me.' She wanted to hear voices as she drifted off to sleep. She didn't want to be alone.

'What about?' Tarin added another branch to the fire and stared into the flames. 'I don't know what to say.' A wolf pup edged closer to the fire and settled down between them. Tarin rested his hand in the soft fur around the wolf's neck.

'Tell me more about your father and the cave lion. What happened next?' She reached for Luuka's hand and held it close. Already the tea was making her feel drowsy.

Tarin collected his thoughts.

'Isto claimed the cave lion. His spear had killed it, so by hunter's right, it was his. But he gave my father a token – one of its teeth. And Kalle had the tooth made into a necklace for my mother.'

Tarin's eyes closed and he pictured the necklace hanging around Aila's neck.

'Hanno drilled a small hole at the base of the tooth, and Salla threaded it onto a thin leather thong. She also threaded pieces of amber and small circles of bone. Kalle told her it was payment for all the worry he had caused her, and she said in that case she would look forward to many more pieces of jewellery in the future.'

Kaija laughed, a small, sleepy chuckle. 'Keep talking. I like to hear your stories. Tell me about your Summer grounds. Do you travel there every year?'

'Most years. It takes us over half the moon's cycle to reach the Summer grounds, and sometimes we stop to trade with other clans along the way. Sometimes, another clan will travel with us. More hunters mean more successful hunts, and to hunt the mammoths, many strong men and women are needed.'

'I've never seen a mammoth.' Kaija yawned and struggled to keep her eyes open. 'Keep talking.'

'Sometimes, even one of the forest clans joins us. It's a chance to trade, and meet with friends and family. We have games and competitions, big feasts, music and dancing.'

'That sounds so nice.'

'Don't the forest clans have a Summer camp?' Tarin asked, surprised. The Mammutti clans moved where the hunting was best – north in summer to hunt the mammoths, then returning south in autumn, in time to gather the fruits, nuts and berries of the forests, and harvest the rich grains, barley and rye from the plains. They fished the rivers for salmon, trout and grayling. Food was dried, frozen under rock caches, and stored in holes dug deep into the ground.

'The Metsamaa? Possibly. I'm not sure.' She yawned again and closed her eyes. She could no longer feel the throbbing in her shoulders. 'I think some do, but River Clan prefers to keep to itself.' She lapsed into silence, then murmured, 'Tell me more.'

She held Luuka's hand to her cheek. His skin was rough and warm. She breathed in his scent. She could no longer keep her eyes open and Tarin's voice was fading softly away.

If I don't wake, Luuka, don't mourn for me. I'll be with Retu, and Mara. Kaija breathed deeply, and slipped into a deep, deep sleep.

Tarin's story continued.

'Last year we travelled to White Fox camp, far to the north. And the year before that, it was Musk Ox camp. It took us nearly a moon cycle just to reach there. If I don't make it to the mountains by Winter, I'm to stay with Musk Ox Clan . . .' His voice faded.

He wasn't going to reach the mountain by winter. It was already winter, and he was further away than when he started. And what was left of the Offering anyway? One cave bear tooth, an amber bead, and a flint blade.

And the beads? Kaija hadn't told him about the beads yet, but Tarin could guess. She'd traded them for Broda's help. He might have done the same thing. That must have been what she was trying to tell him before. He listened to

276

Kaija's breathing. It was slow and regular.

'I think she's asleep,' Luuka whispered. 'Kaija?'

He rubbed the back of her hand, but it sat loosely in his grasp. Slowly, Tarin reached for the blade.

It was heavy in his hands, and cold to touch. Tarin admired the delicate shape and tapered edge. It was one of the finest, sharpest blades Jarkko had ever made. Tarin remembered him choosing the flint so carefully, and sitting cross-legged by the fire, chipping and shaping the stone, little by little. He could still see him turning the stone in his hands, examining it critically, removing another tiny sliver, until he was finally satisfied. Then he handed it to Tarin, placing it into his care, as a mother would surrender her child – proudly, fearfully.

It was a blade fit for the Earth Mother, but now, it would no longer be hers. It would be Kaija's blade. Twice, Kaija had rescued him – once from the river, and then again from Boar Clan. Twice, he owed her his life. He tightened his grip on the knife and felt the blade bite into his skin.

'Mother, what if I fail?'

The cry rose in his throat. He wished his mother was there with him, to tell him what to do. He clasped his pendant to stop his hands from trembling and sent a silent plea to Owl to steady his hand and give courage to his heart. And to Wolf, that strange new protector that had helped him face the Spirits and chase the darkness away.

Kaija stirred in her sleep, and Tarin knew they could delay no longer.

Luuka unwound the bandage and his hand shook as her tunic stuck to the ugly wound. He pulled it free, and she began to bleed again.

'The blood will wash away some of the evil Spirits,' Tarin said. He probed the area around the wound and wiped away the blood.

'Can you feel it?' Luuka asked.

Tarin shook his head. 'It will be small . . .'

A wolf pup whimpered. Tarin lowered the flint blade to Kaija's shoulder, and pressed, drawing a line across her skin. Blood welled beneath the blade and Luuka wiped it away with the remains of the fox furs.

Kaija moaned, the pain reaching her even in her sleep. Tarin thought he might have to cut further, but then he felt a hardness in her flesh that shouldn't be there. He used the tip of the flint knife to prise the jagged spike of bone from the wound. It glistened with blood.

'So small,' Luuka murmured. 'It is all the evil Spirits needed to take her Spirit.' He shuddered and dropped the bone to the ground.

Kaija's shoulder was still bleeding. Tarin bathed the wound with the horsetail wash and bandaged it firmly with a strip of leather. He thought the colour in her face looked better, and she breathed more easily.

'You did a good job, Tarin,' Luuka said. 'Better than I could have done.'

Tarin released a shuddering breath and looked down at his blood-stained hands. Kaija's blood. 'I need to wash,' he said, and retraced his steps to the river. Streaks of pink light now coloured the sky. The river water was icy as Tarin splashed it over his face and neck.

'I did it,' he thought in surprise. He had removed the splinter of bone that was festering in Kaija's shoulder. He had cleaned and bound the wound. He took a long drink of water and stared at the river as it flowed past. But more than that, he thought, he had faced the Spirits, all by himself. No, not all by himself, he amended. He had Owl and Wolf with him.

He splashed his face once more and returned to the fire. One of the pups opened a sleepy eye, then sighed deeply and slept again. Luuka raised an eyebrow at him and handed him a fresh cup of mayweed tea.

'This was the last of your herbs. Even I know what mayweed smells like.'

They drank in silence as the light grew around them.

'Is this the last of your Offering? I'm sorry,' Luuka said.

Tarin swallowed his tea. It tasted good. 'I have an amber

bead from Ilmi and a cave bear tooth.' A wolf pup came looking for food and Tarin pulled it into his lap, stroking its fur. It felt warm and alive. 'I will still go to the Mountain, Luuka,' he said. 'I owe Mammoth Clan that much.' He stared up at the sky as the last stars twinkled faintly. 'Kaija said she would guide me.'

Luuka paused digging at the fire and looked up. 'Kaija said that?'

Tarin nodded. 'When we first met. She said if I helped her rescue you, she would guide me to the Mountain.' Tarin held the cup out to Luuka to share and grinned. 'I would have helped her anyway. Eventually.'

Luuka nodded but remained silent.

'You should sleep some more,' Tarin said. 'Your arm will heal faster if you sleep.'

'Later,' Luuka said. He scratched the other wolf pup who had come looking for food. 'No food now,' he said. 'When Kaija wakes, we'll move further downriver. Perhaps today we can fish. Would you like some fish?' The pup sneezed and went back to sleep. 'Tarin, I should tell you . . . when you were with the Spirits . . .' He stopped and scratched his chin. 'You sat there, and hardly breathed, and it didn't seem very long, but maybe I slept off and didn't realise . . .' He paused again and held out his injured arm. 'But I felt my pain ease. I'm sure of it. The fire in my arm faded and

I know the wounds will heal. You saved us both. Thank you.'

'Thank Spirit of Wolf,' said Tarin. 'Wolf chased away the evil Spirits and showed me how to heal Kaija. I told you that you were now marked by Wolf.'

Luuka smiled. 'Then that's what we'll call ourselves. We need a new name for our new clan. We need to journey together, you, me, Kaija and the pups.'

Tarin nodded slowly. 'A new name for a new clan.'

He thought of his Mammutti family, so far away. How he wished he could tell Aila he was still alive. And Tuuli and Saara. Even Kalle would be proud of him. And Taavo? Taavo wouldn't believe that his weak little brother had survived so many dangers. He imagined sitting by the fire pit, telling his tales to Saara, her eyes growing bigger and rounder. And Old Father – he wanted to tell Valo he had walked in the Spirit World, and that Valo was wrong about so many things.

So many things to tell. So many stories.

But the mammoths were far away, and he would never see them again. A lump settled in his chest and made it hurt. The pup in his lap stirred and sighed. Tarin stroked it, and in the gentle touch of his hands they both found comfort. Kaija was sleeping soundly now, a deep, healing sleep. The shadow had lifted from her wounds. Luuka was staring at the fire and his eyelids were drooping. Soon he would sleep, and that would be best for him. Tarin would watch over them all as they slept.

This is my clan now.

The thought gave him hope.

All of us hurt and injured. All of us grieving and scared. But somehow together, we have become a clan. We have escaped from Boar Clan, and we are still alive.

Tarin's fingers melted into the wolf's soft fur.

We are now Wolf Clan.

Above him, an owl winged silently homewards. He followed its flight until he could see it no longer.

And Owl still protects me, he thought. Owl will always protect me. As Spirit Keeper of this new clan, I ask that Owl protects us wherever we may journey. For us, this Clan of Wolves, the journey has only just begun.

Tarin's World

The setting of this novel is 30,000 years ago, when ice covered all of modern-day Scandinavia, but I have used the forests and *tundra* of Lapland as my inspiration for Tarin's home. Mammoth Clan and River Clan all have Finnish names and are pronounced with a soft 'j', so Kaija becomes 'Kaiya' and Jarkko becomes 'Yarkko.'

Finnish and Saami language

Saami are the traditional Lapland people, spreading across northern Finland, Sweden and Norway. Following are some Finnish and Saami words used in this book:

+ *Kaamos* – a Finnish word relating to polar night. It refers to the months between December and January, when the sun doesn't rise at all. There is gentle light from about 1000 hours to 1400 hours and twilight is long. This word is still in use today.

+ *Mammutti* – Finnish for 'mammoth'.

+ *Haamu* – Finnish for 'ghost'.

+ *Beaska* – a Saami word for a traditional reindeer skin coat. Tarin's *beaska* is actually made of mammoth fur (an author's creative licence).

+ *Tundar* – a Saami word for 'tundra'.

+ *Baybaka* – a Saami word for 'marmot' or 'suslik'.

+ *Giron* – a Saami word for 'rock ptarmigan'.

+ *Pettu* – the layer between bark and wood in the pine, elm or aspen tree. It needs to be mixed with something to be palatable, but it's a source of food in lean times, even today.
+ *Nilkka* – from the Finnish for 'sock'. because of the dark band around her foot.
+ *Rohkea* – Finnish for 'brave'.

Derived words

+ *Metsamaa* – from the Finnish *metsa* (forest) and *maa* (land).
+ *Esi* – from the Saami *Esi-isa* (ancestor).
+ *Mustara* – a made-up herb. From the Finnish *musta* (black). Mustara literally translates as a short version of 'black bird' *(mustarastas)*.

Mammutti Clans live on the tundra and grasslands. Clans include:

+ Mammoth, Saiga, Bison, Musk Ox, White Fox, Wolf, Elk, Reindeer, Cave Lion, Aurochs.

Metsamaa Clans are forest dwellers. Clans include:

+ River (1st Cave, 2nd Cave), Boar, Deer, Lynx, Raven, Cave Bear, Otter, Beaver.

Acknowledgments

I owe my thanks to many people within the Australian writing community, but I would like to pay tribute to a special few who have inspired me, taught me, wiped my tears, and sometimes screamed at me during the evolution of *Tarin of the Mammoths*.

First, Dr Kim Wilkins. It was during her 'Year of the Novel' course at Queensland Writers Centre that I wrote the earliest version of Tarin's story. Her generosity of spirit and her enthusiasm for the craft of writing inspires me every day.

I also extend my thanks to Marele Day. I was fortunate enough to win a mentorship with Marele through the Northern Rivers Writers Centre, and another version of *Tarin* was honed and polished.

For her friendship and warmth, Dr Kate Forsyth. We

meet only rarely, but I learn something new and wonderful each time we talk.

Thanks also to my dear friend, Tina M Clark, for your support, your encouragement and your wise words. Not only has Tina been a true friend over the years, but she is the driving force behind the CYA Later Alligator Conference held each year in Brisbane. It was entirely due to this conference that I first made contact with Penguin Random House and had the opportunity of submitting my manuscript to them.

Enormous thanks go to my editor, Katrina Lehman, for your infinite patience and finding the magic buried within my story.

To Nicole Cody, for showing me a way through the shadows, much love and gratitude.

To the members of SCBWI, the Society of Children's Book Writers and Illustrators – what a fabulous bunch of people you are!

And finally, I come to my husband, Sarj, and my boys, Chris and Alex. I am truly blessed to have you in my life and am filled with gratitude every day that you have chosen to walk with me on my journey. My life is richer because you are here, and it is to you that I dedicate this book.

About the Author

Growing up, Jo Sandhu was sure she was going to be a Shakespearean actress or a pianist, and gained her Associate Diploma in Speech and Drama. However, on leaving school she spent a year in Finland as a Rotary Exchange Student before returning to Australia and working in banking and HR. These days she is a writer, a personal carer, and volunteers at her sons' sporting clubs.

Her short stories have been highly commended in numerous competitions, including the FAW Mary Grant Bruce Award for Children's Literature, and the CYA Later Alligator Competition (Brisbane) in both the Children's and YA sections. She is a member of Queensland Writers Centre and the Society of Children's Book Writers and Illustrators.

Jo currently lives in the Tweed Valley in Northern NSW with her family, and enjoys cooking, travelling and reading.